# UNACCEPTABLE BEHAVIOR

MORGANNA WILLIAMS

Copyright © 2016 by Morganna Williams

Published by Stormy Night Publications and Design, LLC.
www.StormyNightPublications.com

Cover design by Korey Mae Johnson
www.koreymaejohnson.com

Images by 123RF/Claude Belanger

All rights reserved.

1st Print Edition. February 2016

ISBN-13: 978-1523995066

ISBN-10: 1523995068

FOR AUDIENCES 18+ ONLY

This book is intended for adults only. Spanking and other sexual activities represented in this book are fantasies only, intended for adults.

# CHAPTER ONE

Max rushed past the security desk in a panic. She was late for the third time this week.

One of these days, she promised herself, she would get her act together and manage to get out the front door on time consistently.

She'd always been late; in fact, it ran in her family.

"Late again, young lady?"

Max made a face at the deep rumbling tone from directly behind her and turned to frown up at Rafe Jennings, the head of security at OmniCorp. "Don't mess with me, buddy. It's already been a bad morning!" she snapped.

One dark brow rose incredulously at her tone, but he didn't say a word. Instead he simply crossed his arms over the broad expanse of his chest and looked down at her.

She sighed. It was her own fault she was late and there was no reason to take her frustrations out on Rafe. He was one of her favorite people in the building, and truth be told, she found him immeasurably attractive—not that the sentiment would ever be returned. Max was all too aware of how unattractive the opposite sex found her short, pudgy figure.

"I'm sorry, Rafe; it's been a bad morning. I realized when

I went to put my wash in the dryer that I washed my cell phone last night. I spent so much time on the phone with AT&T this morning, I didn't make it out of the apartment until eight-fifteen," she offered in the way of an explanation.

"You don't think it would have been a better choice to call after you got to work on your morning break?"

Max snapped her teeth together with a frustrated click. "Possibly," she said succinctly. "I guess we all live and learn!"

She gave him another glare before turning away from the security desk and sailing down the hall with an exaggerated sniff of disdain.

· · · · · · ·

Rafe bit back a laugh as she snapped the last bit out before sticking her cute upturned nose in the air and spinning away from him. Her green eyes had practically shot sparks.

Maxine Reynolds was one spunky woman. He loved the way her black knee-length skirt hugged her full bottom. His little Max was blessed with some delightful curves—from her large full breasts to the delicious bottom that seemed to beg for his attention.

He'd been flirting with her for months but was beginning to think it would take a sledgehammer to make her realize it. One way or another though, little Miss Maxine's days as a free agent were numbered.

Rafe had tried to be patient and let her get used to his friendship, but it was past time to start laying plans in place. She was too pretty to remain free for long and he didn't want another guy poaching his girl. Max also needed a firm hand to help ground her and keep her organized and he was just the man for the job.

He wondered how she'd respond to a good spanking. Would she run screaming for the hills at the mere suggestion, or would her eyes glaze over and heat with desire? Rafe groaned under his breath and readjusted his trousers as he realized the effect his thoughts were having on his cock.

It was definitely time to stake his claim.

• • • • • • •

Max came into the building and immediately searched the security desk for Rafe; she grinned when he looked up at her with a smile. "Look, Rafe! Isn't my new phone cute! I love it! Best of all I can surf the Internet much faster and open some pretty large files. It's great! And it's *red!*"

Rafe stood and grinned down into her pretty smiling face. "Yes, red is a really good color for you, Maxine."

She made a face. "How many times do I have to tell you to call me Max?"

Rafe tapped a finger lightly on the end of her nose. "I like Maxine."

Max blew a strawberry blond curl out of her eyes and frowned. "Maxine is a blue-haired old lady holding a cigarette in one hand and a malt duck in the other."

"Maxine is a pretty little sprite with strawberry curls and big green eyes who needs to get her butt to work on time," he said firmly.

Max blinked. He was making fun of her! Heat crept up her neck and tears of mortification filled her eyes as she realized he knew how she felt. He knew she thought he was sex on a stick with a capital S and was laughing at her about it!

"Rafe, that was just plain mean!" she yelled up at him before turning and hurrying away to her cubicle. He didn't have to rub her face in the fact that a Greek god such as himself would never be interested in the likes of her. She knew he was out of her league. It wouldn't take a rocket scientist to figure that out, for goodness' sake. But to tease her about her crush was horrid! Max sniffled; she'd really thought Rafe was better than that.

Her shoulders slumping dejectedly, Max sank down in her office chair. Then she remembered her pretty red phone and almost laughed with glee as she remembered her phone could surf the Internet and she could access her account at Amazon—so she could read stories of love and romance with men who weren't afraid to take the plucky heroines in hand, quite literally.

If she wanted to, she could even read stories at her desk. No one would know. After all, a little pick-me-up was warranted after Rafe had been so mean.

Of course, she hadn't counted on so thoroughly losing track of time by continually reading just one more chapter. Before she knew it, she'd 'just one more chapter-ed' through lunch and the better part of the afternoon. Max flushed guiltily as she realized she'd accomplished absolutely no work all day.

*It's not as if I am not one of the best workers here most the time,* she thought to herself in an effort to excuse her behavior.

Her face flushed again and her bottom tingled as she thought of the three delicious stories she'd read that day. Each and every one of them had featured a no-nonsense hero who spanked the daylights out of his heroine repeatedly.

Max couldn't help but picture herself over Rafe's strong thighs. The thought made her shiver.

Even though she was a big girl, he made her feel small. Rafe was at least 6'4" with wide shoulders, a broad chest that tapered neatly down to muscular hips and thighs. Add the coal black hair and deep blue eyes and he was enough to get any woman's heart beating double time.

She gave a despondent little sigh. Rafe was the homecoming king type and Max knew she was so not homecoming queen material.

*No sense stewing about it,* she thought, then grinned as the clock flashed five. The day really sped by when you were goofing off.

On her way home she hit so many red lights, Max looked

thoughtfully at her phone. Surely it wouldn't hurt to read a little at the lights. After all, it wasn't like she would be moving, just sitting.

Once the idea occurred to her, Max couldn't resist. She spent every red light on the way home emerged in another tale of spanking delight.

In fact, she was enjoying the drive so much more than usual, Max drove around her apartment block four times to finish the current chapter she was reading.

• • • • • • •

Rafe smiled across the desk at his boss and friend, Tom Brooks. They'd gone to college together and when Rafe had finally had enough of the politics involved in working for the CIA and was ready to go into the private sector, Tom needed someone to head up his security department.

Rafe had been with Tom for over a year and never regretted his decision to sign on. When Max was hired a few months ago, it was the icing on the cake.

They usually got together after work every Monday to have a drink in Tom's office and discuss any security issues that had arisen the week before. He grinned as Tom pulled out the single malt Scotch and poured them each a healthy dose.

The business part of their meeting was over and they were just remembering when they'd been freshmen at Texas A&M. They'd been so green they could've grown corn in their ears.

Tom suddenly got a serious look on his face. "Do you know what's going on with Max?" He'd seen the writing on the wall between his old friend and his research clerk.

Rafe frowned. "What do you mean?"

"She's always been a great worker but the last week or so, her productivity has really slipped. I can usually count on Max to put out the work of three people and lately she's barely managing to finish anything and nothing on time. It's not at all like her and I don't really want to write her up. She's a sensitive little thing."

"You want me to find out what's going on and talk to her about it?"

"Yes. I don't want to have to go to any disciplinary action. I just want my dependable Max back. If you talk to her, I can just pretend we never had this conversation and her career won't be affected," Tom reasoned.

"I really appreciate your giving me the chance to deal with this, Tom. I know Max's career means a lot to her," Rafe said softly, wondering what had gotten into the little minx. "You want me to talk to her about being on time while I'm at it?"

Tom laughed. "I don't want to push my luck. I'm not sure anything can help Max in that department." Rafe laughed with him and shook his head. He had a feeling he could work wonders with Miss Maxine but he would keep that thought to himself.

• • • • • • •

Rafe frowned as he watched Max at her desk. She didn't seem to be doing anything but staring at her phone. What in the world was she doing?

He cleared his throat and watched her start guiltily, punch a few buttons, and stick her phone in her pocket before turning to her computer with a studious look.

"What are you doing, Maxine?" he asked in a stern voice.

Max nearly jumped a mile. "N-nothing... I was working."

A dark brow rose almost into his hairline. "Looked to me like you were playing with your phone."

She glared up at him. "I was just answering a text from my sister, Mr. Nosy."

"Hmmmm," was all he said before walking back toward his own office. He had been watching Max off and on for a couple of days and all he'd ever seen her do when she didn't think anyone was watching was stare at that phone.

He shook his head and decided he'd keep giving her rope because it was only a matter of time before she hung herself. He wondered how long it would take her to get in a situation beyond her control; one that would enable him to step in and seize the day, so to speak. He never expected it to happen on his way home from work that very day.

Rafe looked in his rearview mirror at the driver of the compact little Chevy Sport and realized Max didn't even know she was behind him at the light; she was too focused on whatever was in her lap.

When the car to her right loudly honked, he watched in horror as Max jumped and gunned the gas; there was little he could do except brace for impact.

*Crunch!!*

He climbed down from the cab and hurried to check on Maxine; she was just getting out of her car and obviously shaken.

"Rafe, I'm so sorry… I…" she began tearfully.

"Are you okay?" he asked, grasping her lightly by the shoulders and giving her a once-over.

Max nodded miserably, then she looked at the front of her car and looked like she was about to burst into tears. It was completely crumpled in like tissue paper. Rafe's chrome bumper didn't look bad at all, just a few scratches and streaks of orange paint. Then she pointed to the green fluid running out of her car.

"What's that?"

"Transmission fluid," Rafe said with a frown as he walked to the driver's door of her car. He decided just to be safe he'd better turn it off and when he leaned in to do just that, a light from the floorboard drew his attention. Closer inspection revealed her pretty little red phone. He frowned as he noticed the words on the screen; he read a few lines as he picked it up and whistled. Someone named Jack was whaling the tar out of a girl named Amanda's butt.

It was a spanking story. A grin lit his face as he locked

the screen on Maxine's phone and dropped it into his shirt pocket. *Isn't this ironic?* he thought to himself and wondered if Max would eventually appreciate the irony of her situation.

# CHAPTER TWO

Max bit her lip as she watched Rafe take charge of the situation; almost before she could blink he'd called one of his security guards to come help push her car out of the way of oncoming traffic and hustled her into the cab of his big truck. While she waited for Rafe to get in the truck, she contemplated what had just happened; her heart was still beating ninety to nothing from the scare. Thank God Rafe was okay.

She'd been reading about a feisty young lady getting her bare bottom spanked first with the hero's hand and then his belt. When the horn honked, Max thought the light was green and gunned it only to crash into the back of the big Dually truck in front of her, and was mortified to look up and see the light was still red.

What if she'd hurt someone? She was so *stupid!* Her heart had nearly dropped to her feet when a frowning Rafe climbed down from the cab; of all the people to rear-end. Could this day get any worse?

Rafe climbed into the seat next to her and put his truck in gear; without a word he pulled up and parked in front of the office building.

"Ummm... I guess I should..." Max began hesitantly.

"What you should do is go up and wait for me in my office, young lady," he said in a no-nonsense tone.

Max blinked as she studied his usually easygoing face. Rafe looked different… he looked stern. "I'm really sorry about…"

"Go wait in my office, Maxine. When I get your car towed I'll come up to you and we can have a little talk about how sorry you are."

"Rafe…"

"Now!" The sharp command sent her flying from his truck and into the building. She suddenly felt the need to get as far away from him as possible. His very tone made her bottom clench and tingle in the oddest way, which was silly of course. Rafe would never dare to do such a thing as spank her. Would he? Max flushed as her clit seemed to jolt to throbbing attention at just the thought and telltale moisture sprang forth to moisten the gusset of her panties.

She sighed as she unlocked the front door to their offices. It was so quiet it when it was empty it was almost creepy. By ten after five the whole building was completely cleared out unless something special was going on. Tom the CEO felt very strongly about keeping work and home balanced so everyone generally hit the doors right at five.

Max looked nervously into the dark interior of Rafe's office. "This is silly!" she said to herself, but acknowledged that it felt a little like being sent to the principal's office.

The more she thought about Rafe's highhanded attitude, the more irritated Max became. It wasn't like she rear-ended him on purpose! There was no reason to be so nervous and she decided she had no intention of waiting for Rafe in his office like a naughty child. Her cubicle would do just fine.

Her shoulders set in a firm line, she marched down to her little cubicle and turned on the light. Looking at the stack of work she'd been ignoring for the last week or so, Max sighed. Maybe if she did penance by working on some of it, she wouldn't feel as guilty about hitting Rafe.

In a matter of minutes Max was absorbed in her work,

determined to accomplish something while she waited.

• • • • • • •

Rafe gave a satisfied nod as he watched his little troublemaker hightail it out of sight; hopefully she was beginning to grasp the seriousness of her situation. He knew it would take a while to get a tow truck, then to take care of setting it up with a reputable mechanic. While he took care of business, little Miss Maxine could stew in her juices.

He contemplated the opportunity that Max herself had just handed him on a silver platter; Rafe had been wondering how to engineer a discipline situation and she'd done it all on her own. He found himself grinning as he talked to the garage he regularly used for his own truck. It was another forty-five minutes before the tow truck came and her car was loaded. She'd had plenty of time to think about her actions.

It was time to pay the piper! He grinned and headed into the office building.

Rafe frowned when he walked into his dark, empty office. Someone was really looking for a sore bottom.

"Maxine!"

• • • • • • •

Max jumped. "Down here, Rafe... you don't have to roar!"

"I thought I was pretty clear with my instructions, young lady." The soft-spoken words from directly behind her sent a shiver of foreboding across Max's skin.

"I just thought I would..."

"I don't know what you just thought but I know you better get your keister down the hall to my office pronto, little girl." Again the command was given quietly and somehow it was way scarier to Max than if he'd yelled.

"Rafe, I know I really screwed up but..."

"One…"

She blinked. He was counting?

"Two…"

Max's eyes widened and she rubbed her hands over her arms to dispel the shivery feeling that seemed to be growing.

"Three…"

She jumped up and hurried down the hallway to Rafe's office. Max wasn't exactly sure what was happening but childhood had ingrained the knowledge that anything higher than three was really bad.

Her heart was pounding in her chest as she skidded to a stop and plopped down into the chair in front of his big desk.

The light flickered on behind her. Max held her breath with an air of expectancy. She had no idea what she was expecting, but the way her tummy was doing flip-flops said it wasn't good.

Strong thighs came into view as Rafe seated himself on the edge of his desk in front of her. Max gulped.

"Look at me, young lady." Again with the soft-spoken command.

Max stared straight ahead, afraid of what she'd see in his eyes if she looked up. He would surely hate her now.

"Maxine…" he drawled slowly, as if to wring every ounce of displeasure with her he could from the two syllables.

Max looked up to meet his eyes. The stern look that met her caused her bottom to clench of its own volition.

"You want to tell me what happened out there?"

"I rear-ended you?"

One dark brow rose.

"It was an accident…"

"What were you doing when you had the accident?"

"Ummm… well, I guess I was… changing the radio station… yes, changing the radio station and only took my eyes off the road for a second and…" Max was warming to her explanation.

"You wanna try again?"

Max frowned. "No, I just told you what happened..." Her stomach plummeted from about twenty stories when he pulled her cell phone from his shirt pocket. *Please let it have gone dead... please.*

"Now it seems to me you were reading a story about a girl named Amanda getting her butt busted," Rafe said baldly.

So much heat filled her face, Max thought she would spontaneously combust at any moment. This was mortifying.

"You wanna tell me what Miss Amanda did to warrant such discipline?"

She didn't answer but watched Rafe put a finger to the side of his face as he pretended to think about it.

"Hmmmm, what could she have done...? Could she have been reading while driving and rear-ended Jack?"

All that Max could manage with the huge lump in her throat was a horrified squeak and a shake of her head in response.

"Cat got your tongue?"

She closed her eyes as even more heat rushed up her neck and a pounding started in her ears. Max wondered if it was possible to expire due to embarrassment then realized she couldn't be that lucky. "She forgot to pay the water bill," she said softly.

Rafe took a minute to admire her color-infused face before getting up to get the straight-backed desk chair by the window. Setting it down a few feet from Max, he rolled up his sleeves.

Max finally risked opening her eyes when the silence grew too long to bear. The sight of the chair and Rafe rolling up his sleeves made her shoot straight up in her seat.

"Wh-what are you doing?"

"What does it look like?"

She decided to do the only sensible thing and run. Unfortunately she didn't even make it to the door before

Rafe was standing in front of it blocking her exit, so she pivoted sharply and ran to the other side of the desk to put it between them.

"Come here, Maxine," Rafe said softly as he stalked slowly around the desk, while she circled in the opposite direction, making sure to keep the desk between them.

"No way, José," she said with a shake of her head.

"You aren't leaving this office without the discipline you and I both know you deserve," he said firmly just before he vaulted over the desk, landing lightly on his feet right in front of her.

Max screamed and made another mad dash to the door in an effort to escape her fate but he caught her with ease.

"Uh, uh, uh," he said as he caught her around the waist and hauled her to the chair, managing to sit down and pull her down over his thighs in almost one movement. "You and I have some business to settle, little lady."

"You can't!" she wailed, trying to twist away from him to no avail.

Rafe simply rested his broad palm on her upturned bottom and asked, "Can't do what?"

She froze over his lap. Good night, Irene! He was going to make her say it out loud!

"I can't do what, Maxine?" The velvet-encased steel was back in his voice.

"You can't… you can't…" She stopped, near tears, helplessly hanging over his knees.

"Can't what?"

Finally she slumped in defeat, knowing Rafe would wait until she said it. "Spank me." She sniffed miserably.

"With pleasure," he said with a grin and began pulling up her skirt to reveal the target area.

"No! I said you can't spank me!" she screamed.

"I could have sworn I just heard your sweet voice ask me to spank you."

"C-A-N-T, I said you *can't* spank me!" she yelled in alarm.

"Watch me, little girl," Rafe said, dispensing with her skirt and panties almost before she knew what was happening.

Max hadn't thought her embarrassment could get worse, but that was before she realized he was looking down at her humongo bare bottom.

"No, Rafe!"

"Yes, Maxine. I think you deserve at least as much as Miss Amanda got, don't you?" he asked almost conversationally as he skimmed a hand lightly across her bottom almost as if he liked what he saw…

She started squirming almost desperately, trying in vain to get away. "Stop!"

"Stop? I haven't even started. Don't be so impatient," he scolded before lifting his hand and smacking it back down on her posterior.

Her whole body jerked in response. "Owwww!"

Rafe tucked her in tight and began to deliver a thorough and blistering hand spanking. Max was still yelling 'no' into about the twentieth smack; by the thirtieth she was simply yelping in tune to whatever beat was playing in his head.

Max couldn't believe how much it hurt! He paid special attention to the tender area where her bottom met her thighs, leaving her wailing over his lap. He was lighting a fire she knew would last awhile.

By the time Rafe felt she'd had enough, her bottom was a brilliant scarlet from the top of her bottom to midway down her thighs. Max was a sniffling mess when he stood her up in front of him.

She shifted from foot to foot, trying to wriggle the awesome sting out of her behind.

"Look at me, Maxine," he said sternly.

She shook her head.

"Max… one…" Her head flew up when he started counting and she saw him bite back a smile; the brute found her predicament amusing! "What do you think about reading while you're driving now?"

"I'll never do it again!" she promised fervently.

"Hmmm… I think you should do some corner time and think about what led you to this moment," Rafe said, standing to guide her over to the corner nearest the door.

"I don't want to…" A slap to her already tenderized rear stopped the small rebellion in its tracks.

"I didn't ask if you wanted to, young lady," he said in a firm, no-nonsense tone.

Max soon found herself standing bare-bottomed, nose in the corner with a flaming backside. As she stood there sniffling, she wanted to rant and rave about the injustice of it, but knew deep down the spanking was deserved. The thought of what she'd done to Rafe of all people made her want to weep anew.

Forget dating; now he wouldn't even be her friend. While she'd known she really didn't stand a chance with the handsome head of security, at least until now, Max had been able to keep her fantasy alive. But now, she felt its loss keenly.

Still, she knew crying over it would have to wait until she was alone in her apartment. *Besides, I have enough to cry about at the moment,* she realized as she reached back to rub her scorched bottom.

Before she even touched it, her hand was intercepted and another sharp smack landed on her tender cheeks. "No rubbing."

She'd been so wrapped up in her thoughts that Max hadn't even realized Rafe was still standing right behind her. Her humiliation was complete; not only had he spanked her bare bottom, he was standing behind her watching it jiggle as she tried in vain to wag some of the sting out of it. She felt her shoulders slump in defeat and a deep sigh sounded behind her.

Max gasped when she heard the sound of his belt sliding through pant loops and she spun around to face him, pressing her belabored bottom to the corner as if to protect it.

"No, Rafe! Please… I can't take anymore," she wailed passionately.

"You can and will take every bit of what you've earned, Maxine. I told you I thought it would be just deserts for you to get exactly what Amanda got in the story and she finished with a taste of the belt," he said resolutely.

Max felt her face blanch. Amanda had finished with twenty-five licks of Jack's belt. She knew for sure because she'd read the scene through at least eight times. It was hard to believe that earlier today she'd found it a delicious scene to read, because now Max didn't think she'd ever read another spanking story as long as she lived. Reality had a lot more bite!

"Bend over the edge of my desk, Maxine," Rafe said quietly.

She studied his face, looking for any softening of his features. There was none and Max knew she needed to buck up and take whatever punishment he gave her.

Under his stern gaze she marched up to the desk and laid her torso across it, telling herself she was woman enough to take her punishment. A wistful little thought of what it would be like to always answer to Rafe this way made her shiver a little.

"Good girl, I'm proud of you," he told her after she'd positioned herself.

Max was shocked by the swell of pride that filled her at his words. She watched over her shoulder as Rafe doubled the belt in his hand and placed a hand on the small of her back to hold her in place. "Twenty-five and we'll be done."

Max closed her eyes; she'd known it was too much to hope for that he hadn't actually read the scene. Her eyes flew back open the instant the first line of fire fell across her vulnerable backside.

The next ten fell in quick succession; obviously Rafe didn't want to drag this out.

Max was gasping for air as his belt left unbelievable heat in its wake. Another ten fell rapidly across the tops of her thighs.

Max sobbed across the desk. "I'm sorreeee… please… I'm sorreeee…"

Rafe applied the last five to her sit spots almost one right on top of the other, then dropped the belt to scoop her up into his arms. "Shhhhhh, baby, it's okay. It's all over."

He crooned softly as he carried her to his big desk chair and sat with her cuddled in his lap. Max wrapped her arms around him and sobbed into his neck. "I'm sorry, Rafe… I know I was stupid…"

"Shhhh… all is forgiven." He continued to rub her back and kiss the top of her head until she calmed down.

Max sniffed one more time and then became conscious of the fact that her skirt was still rucked up around her waist and she had no idea where her panties were. She was practically sitting on Rafe's lap naked! Plus she was way too heavy to be sitting on him like this; had he carried her over here? Rafe let her up as soon as she tried to pull away. He watched her almost frantic efforts to pull her skirt down and reached out to help. Embarrassed, Max tried to slap his hands away.

"Maxine." She froze again at the warning in his tone and let him set her skirt to rights.

Rafe tried to pull her back down onto his lap but she resisted. "I'm too heavy."

"I personally think you're just right but that's a conversation for another day; you're tired and we have work tomorrow so I'd better run you home."

Max nodded and walked over to find her purse; her eyes nearly crossed when she spotted her panties by the wall where she'd apparently kicked them during the spanking. Without a word she grabbed them and stuffed them into her purse. "Could I have my phone?"

"No. I'll be keeping that for a week," Rafe said as he guided her out the door.

"I beg your pardon?" she asked incredulously. She finally looked at him with a glare.

"Hmmm, make it two weeks," he said as he pulled her along behind him.

"Two weeks!" Max spluttered as she tried to keep up with his long-legged strides, feeling every step in the hot, tight skin of her roasted behind. "But it's *my* phone!"

"I personally think two weeks without it will give you a little more time to think about what you could have done differently."

"But it's *my* phone!" she yelled again.

Rafe suddenly stopped to look down at her with a raised brow. Max closed her mouth and covered her bottom with her free hand as if to protect it.

He nodded and started pulling her along again. "I was beginning to think we'd left the office too soon. If you argue anymore, Maxine, I'll keep it for three weeks. Understood?"

"Yes," she said softly.

"Excuse me?"

"Yes, sir."

"Better."

Max felt like she was practically trotting to keep up with him but didn't want to complain. Rafe was justified in being angry with her.

For the last hour she'd vacillated between guilt and outrage at his highhanded behavior. Currently her sore bottom was bringing the guilt to the fore and Max wanted nothing more than to go to bed and forget about this terrible day.

Rafe opened the door to his big truck, picked her up, and plopped her right down on the plush seat. Max hissed and shot straight up into the air.

"Owwww! There is no way I can sit for the ride home, I'll walk," she said miserably as she tried to climb down from the truck.

"You sit your bottom right down, young lady," Rafe said firmly. "Sitting on a well-earned sore backside on the way home will help you remember to make better choices in the future."

Max sniffled and sank back down onto the seat with a wince. She was too tired to fuss about it. At least her apartment wasn't very far away.

"Did the garage say how long it would take to fix my car?" she asked.

"Actually the mechanic said it would only be about a week but as far as you're concerned Maxine, your car has been impounded."

"Impounded! What do you mean impounded?" she screeched.

"I mean that as soon as it's fixed, it will be parked in the garage for the next month. You can use the time to really think about your responsibilities as a driver to adhere to rules that provide for your own safety and that of everyone else on the road."

"You can't do this! It's *my* car, I pay for it. I am an adult, not sixteen! You cannot just decide to take my car away from me for my own good!" she yelled, furious at the way Rafe seemed to be making such arbitrary decisions.

Rafe shook his head. "I certainly can, Maxine, and you will follow my rules. Unless of course you'd rather I just call the police and let them handle the situation, although I'm pretty sure once they know the facts, your license will be suspended and you'll be without wheels a lot longer than a month."

The beginnings of fresh tears burned at the backs of her eyes. "I can't believe you're doing this to me."

"Honey, I'm not doing anything but trying to take care of you. You are lucky you escaped with a damaged car today. What if a pedestrian was walking across the street when you hammered down the gas? You'd be sitting in a jail cell while your life fell around you in ruins."

The truth of his words brought a strangled sob from her throat. "How can I be so stupid?"

"You aren't stupid, Maxine. You've just been a little out of control and I aim to help you bring yourself back into line," Rafe said determinedly.

"How do you plan to do that? By beating me?" She snapped the last question.

"I didn't beat you and you know it. If you're honest with yourself, you'll admit I just did what you've needed for a long time now. Or you wouldn't be reading spanking stories."

"That is not your business, Rafe Jennings!"

"I've decided to make it my business and I'm going to tell you right now to lose the attitude. I'm beginning to think I should just pull over and spank you again!"

"No! I'm sorry, Rafe. This has all been a lot to deal with," Max said quietly.

"Which is why I'm cutting you some slack, but you'd do well to remember my patience is not endless, young lady," he said as he pulled up in front of her apartment building. "You get along inside and I'll pick you up at seven-thirty sharp in the morning."

Max nodded. "Thank you for the ride." She got down carefully from her seat to keep from jolting her bottom unduly and made her way inside. Rafe watched her until the light in her apartment came on before pulling away from the curb.

Part of her was relieved he hadn't walked her to the door but another part was disappointed; what if he'd walked her to the door and kissed her senseless? Then he could have rubbed the sting out of her bottom until she was purring and ready to give herself completely to him.

Max shook her head, irritated with herself. "That's a stupid fantasy, Max! Give it up; you will never be the type of girl a guy like Rafe would be interested in." Feeling she'd sufficiently reined in the romantic side of her nature, Max quickly stripped her clothing and climbed into bed. It had been a very long day and all she wanted to do was sleep and escape from the burning pain in her bottom and her silly longings.

## CHAPTER THREE

Maxine was dressed and ready well before the time Rafe appointed for her to be waiting on the curb. As she met her own eyes in the mirror, she began to panic.

She didn't see how she would ever be able to face Rafe again. Not only did she rear-end him, he'd rear-ended her in the worst way by delivering a thorough spanking.

Max knew the real problem wasn't even the spanking; she was barely even sore this morning, which she would never have believed possible last night. The real problem was he'd seen her bare bottom.

All Max could think about was all of the bottoms he'd seen before. Probably model bottoms, homecoming queen bottoms, beauty queen bottoms; she knew her big, wiggly, fleshy bottom would be no comparison to all the stellar bottoms that had gone before. It was humiliating to think how wanting he would have found her posterior.

Added to the fact he now knew all about her favorite reading material and there was no way she'd ever show her face again.

"I'll just have to resign," Max told her reflection morosely.

Fifteen minutes later the doorbell rang. Max had no

doubt who she would find on the other side of the door. She should have been obediently standing on the curb ten minutes ago.

"Maxine! Front and center!" His commanding voice came through the door loud and clear.

"I've decided to resign. It's the best for everyone all the way around," she called back through the door.

"I'm disappointed in you, Maxine. I never figured you for a coward," was his only reply. Then nothing, Max listened at the door for any sounds to indicate he was still there. Looking through the peephole revealed only an empty hallway. Perversely, Max was disappointed and a little disgruntled he'd given up so easily.

With a sniff she cracked open the door and stuck her head out to see if he was really gone. Max nearly fell out into the hall when the door was suddenly pulled all the way open.

"Good, you're dressed for work. Grab your purse and let's go."

"I... I'm not going. I'm going to turn in my resignation effective immediately."

"You'll do nothing of the sort; I'm trying to be patient this morning, Maxine, but you're skating on thin ice. Get your purse and let's go." Rafe looked down at her and the look in his eye told her in no uncertain terms where things would end up if she continued to be difficult.

Max sighed before running inside to grab her purse and following him submissively out to the truck.

Once they were on the road, Rafe looked over to where Max sat looking pensively out the window. "It will all be all right, Maxine."

Horrified, Max felt tears come to her eyes at the tenderly spoken words. She wanted so badly to believe what he said was true.

"We just need to deal with one other little issue and you can start again with a fresh slate. We both can," Rafe said almost conversationally.

She looked over at him in confusion. "What other little

issue?"

He raised that infernal brow again. "The little issue of neglecting your job duties to read at your desk for the last few weeks."

"What!?!" She sat straight up, her face flushing with embarrassment and alarm.

Rafe smiled indulgently. "You know exactly what I'm talking about. Tom talked to me about the decline in your productivity and asked me to get to the bottom of things. I've been watching you, young lady; I just didn't understand your fascination with the new phone until I found it on your floorboard on a spanking story."

"Do you plan to embarrass me for the rest of my life?" she asked crossly. Everything he said was true but the word 'spanking' wasn't something you said out loud, especially to someone else. It was private! The way he kept saying 'spanking' and 'spanking stories' so cavalierly made her feel almost as naked as when her bottom had been across his lap the night before.

"Were you or were you not reading spanking stories at work, young lady?"

"Stop saying that!" she screeched.

"Stop saying what?"

"Sp... spanking," she whispered.

"There's no need to be embarrassed, Maxine. Spanking is not a dirty word."

"Shhh." Max closed her eyes and wondered why she couldn't ever succumb to the vapors and faint. It would be a great way to escape the current conversation.

"Besides, tonight I'm going to be doing a lot more than saying it," Rafe stated matter-of-factly.

Her eyes flew open and she stared across the seat at him. "What do you mean?"

"I mean after work I expect you to present yourself at my office ready to be disciplined for reading instead of working the last few weeks."

"You've got to be kidding," she said in disbelief.

"I think you know good and well I'm not kidding. little girl. Did the spanking I delivered last night feel like I was kidding?"

"Bu-but that was in the heat of the moment... a one-off kind of thing... not something that will happen again," she babbled, and then catching sight of his knowing smirk, Max snapped at him, "I will not allow you to spank me again!"

Rafe merely smiled as he pulled into a parking space. "I wasn't asking your permission, Maxine. I was just explaining what was expected of you. You'll find things go a lot easier if you obey me and take what you've earned."

Max looked at him like he'd sprouted another head and finally just climbed down from the cab without a word and hurried into the building.

At 4:35 p.m., Max called and ordered a cab; promptly at 5 p.m. she shut down her computer and walked to the front of the building where the cabbie waited. She felt good about the quantity and quality of work she'd completed today. Maybe it would make up some for the lackadaisical attitude she'd exhibited of late.

As for presenting herself to Rafe for punishment, Max decided he had no right to expect anything of the kind. He wasn't her boss in any way, shape, or form. He was simply the head of security and she didn't have to answer to him. The note she left on a sticky pad on her desk said as much.

• • • • • • •

Rafe just smiled at her retreating figure. One way or another Maxine would be getting a spanking this evening; it was up to her if it would be just his hand or something a little more intense.

Of course 5 p.m. came and went with no sign of Maxine. He went looking for her and found her work area tidy and obviously closed up for the night.

Rafe nearly laughed out loud when he saw the note on her desk; it simply read,

*You aren't the boss of me!*

He was really looking forward to showing little Miss Maxine just how wrong about that she was as he intended to be the boss of her in every way possible. It was almost time to demonstrate that little fact to her in the most fundamental of ways, but unfortunately, before Rafe could take her to bed and conquer her in the way such things had been decided throughout history, he had to complete her discipline and get it behind them. But once that was out of the way, all bets were off and little Miss Maxine would find herself well and truly claimed.

• • • • • • •

Max was so keyed up by the time she got home, she decided to take a hot, relaxing bath. Soon she was surrounded by smooth jazz as the soft scent of lavender filled the air, enveloping her in its soothing smell as surely as the hot silky water cradled her in its embrace.

By the time she climbed out of the tub, she was as limp as a noodle. She smiled sleepily at her reflection and released her strawberry curls from their precarious perch on top of her head to fall around her flushed face.

Wrapped in her big fuzzy pink robe, Max opened the bathroom door and walked into her bedroom—only to jump and scream at a sudden pounding on the front door.

"Maxine, open this door!" Rafe yelled.

Max marched to the front door. "You go away, Rafe Jennings!"

"Open the door, Maxine, and accept your punishment," he said commandingly.

"I will not!" she cried.

"Either open the door or I'll open it myself," he said softly.

"You will do no such thing!" Max yelled, only to gasp in

shock when the door in question swung open as easily as if he'd had the key. "How did you get in here?" she demanded, outraged by his intrusion. She prudently ignored the large wooden paddle hairbrush he was holding.

Rafe snorted. "I'm a security expert, darlin', getting in here was cake."

"You have no right to barge into my apartment and threaten me!" she fumed. "I have a good mind to call the police."

"I haven't made any threats. I'm just following through on a promise. Now either call the police, or come here," he said firmly as he sat down in the center of her couch.

"No!"

He sighed as if in resignation. "One..."

"Now, Rafe..."

"Two..."

She wanted to scream with frustration but her tummy was turning cartwheels and he was counting again.

"Three..."

Max did the most intelligent thing under the current set of circumstances; she threw herself face down across his lap. "Okay! You win!"

"Good girl, you just reduced your time with the hairbrush by about half," Rafe said approvingly.

"How 'bout no hairbrush at all?" Max asked hopefully.

"Nothing doin', sweetheart; the minute you decided not to do as you were told, the hairbrush became necessary," Rafe explained as he tossed the back of her fuzzy robe to her waist and pulled her in tight.

With no further preamble his broad palm connected smartly with her still damp bottom.

"Owwww!"

"When I tell you to present yourself for a punishment, young lady, I expect you to do exactly that." His hand fell hard and fast as if to punctuate his words. "I don't want to have to hunt you down to give you what you've asked for by your own behavior."

At least twenty more hard smacks fell in quick succession. "If you don't want a spanking, behave like the mature, responsible adult I know you are."

The volley of swats following that salvo were lost to Max as the heat in her backside built to unbelievable proportions. Soon she didn't even hear Rafe's lecture, she was too busy wiggling her bottom in an effort to evade his hard hand.

Not that she was successful; the spanking went on for what seemed like hours, until Max was a limp sobbing mess across his thighs. She hiccupped loudly as he lifted her to stand in front of him.

Her robe remained tucked up into its belt and Rafe stayed her hand when she moved to pull it back down. "Leave it. I find corner time more effective when a young lady stands there with her bare bottom on display."

"But Rafe…"

"The only butt in this situation is yours. Now get your nose in that corner and think about what you could have done differently today to prevent the taste of the hairbrush you're about to get."

Max wailed as he guided her nose into the appointed corner with a slap to her already flaming backside. She'd thought the spanking last night was bad, but this one had been way worse. Max had a feeling she would still feel it plenty come morning this time.

"I don't want a taste of the hairbrush," she said miserably.

"Then you should have been in my office at the appointed time." Not a hint of softness was in his tone.

"Yes, sir."

"If you'd done as you were told, I would have delivered a mild hand spanking much like the one you received last night. Apparently I did you no favors by tempering myself last night. If I'd given you a real licking with that belt, you'd have still felt it this morning and wouldn't have been so quick to disregard my instructions. I won't be making the same mistake tonight."

Her shoulders slumped as the last bit of defiance eked out of her; his words felt like a death knell for her backside. First thing in the morning Max would burn that brush, but that wouldn't do anything to spare her bottom tonight.

"Let's get this over with, Maxine," Rafe said firmly, calling her from the corner.

Max went meekly back over his knee and gasped in alarm when he tipped her further across his left thigh and scissored his right leg over hers. This was going to be bad!

Rafe didn't leave her in suspense; the brush cracked down almost immediately. Soon the room was filled with the sounds of the brush smacking her bottom and her squeals of dismay.

He covered every inch of her cheeks in a methodical manner, then covered every area a second and a third time. Max felt as if every feeling and emotion centered in her throbbing behind. Finally Rafe tilted her over just a little further to finish with a flurry of smacks to her sit spots, leaving Max howling.

"Is this a lesson that will need to be repeated, Maxine?"

"No!!" she wailed.

"Good." Rafe sat her up on his lap, holding her close and rocking her as she calmed.

When her sobs had gentled to the occasional sniffle, he tilted her face up to his. "This spanking was for disobeying me. You still have to deal with your behavior at work."

"I don't want another spanking!" she cried, ready to burst into tears again at the thought of even a feather falling on her bottom.

"Nevertheless, I will expect you in my office promptly at 5 o'clock tomorrow." His tone brooked no argument.

"Please, my bottom already hurts," Max begged.

"As well it should. I'll expect you at 5 o'clock, Maxine. Understood?"

"Rafe…"

"Understood?"

Max heaved a shuddering sigh of defeat and sank back

against his big chest as if seeking comfort. "Yes, sir."

"Good girl. Now climb into bed." Rafe held the covers up for her as Max climbed beneath them; she immediately opted to roll onto her tummy and hissed in her breath when the covers fell across her bottom. It seemed the most natural thing in the world for Rafe to lean across her and press a gentle kiss to her brow before turning out the light and leaving the room.

Max knew she had to be a masochist because more than anything, she wished he'd shed his own clothing, climbed in bed next to her, and held her through the night.

*Like that will ever happen... dream on, Maxine!*

# CHAPTER FOUR

"You've got to be kidding!" Max screeched incredulously at Rafe across the truck cab.

"I am perfectly serious, young lady," Rafe stated firmly.

"I will *not* give you my panties!" she yelled.

"You will either take them off yourself and hand them to me or I will take them. If I have to take them, I'll spank you while I'm in the area," he promised with an arch of his brow.

"I cannot go all day at work without panties! I just can't do it! And I don't understand why you would want me to!" Max felt her face turn bright red and realized she'd blushed more around this man in the last week than the entire rest of her life combined.

"Consider it more of your punishment; every time you feel your skirt slide across your bottom, you'll remember where that bottom is going to be when it's five-oh-two," Rafe said with far too much enthusiasm for her peace of mind.

"It's indecent!"

"No one will know unless you tell them, Maxine. No one but me and one very naughty young lady."

Max felt her bottom clench at those words. "I won't do

it!"

"One…"

Max closed her eyes and hissed with frustration—she hated the counting!

"Two…"

"Stop that right now, Rafe Jennings!" she yelled with false bravado.

"Three… stop stalling, Maxine," he said softly.

"Oh, shut up!" Max wailed as she reached quickly beneath her ankle-length skirt and removed her panties. Thankfully, the length of the skirt preserved her modesty but the thought of not having any panties on all day at work was almost enough to make her expire on the spot! With a murderous glare she threw the offending garment at Rafe's head.

She growled with frustration as the wispy bit of fluff came to rest rather inelegantly on the gear shift. Rafe chuckled. She glared at him; the man knew very well she'd been aiming for his face. He smiled as he tucked the panties into his jacket pocket; Max crossed her arms over her chest and turned to frown moodily out the window.

"That wasn't so hard, was it?" he asked.

Max refused to answer or look up from the window she was busy glaring holes in. He smiled again as he pulled away from the curb.

The drive to work was quick if silent; the minute Rafe parked, Max hopped out of the truck intent on getting away from him to her safe little cubicle.

"Maxine?" Her back stiffened at the demanding way he said her name.

Max turned to face him warily. "Yes?"

"I want you in my office at five o'clock sharp, understand?"

"Yes, sir!" she bit out tightly before spinning away to run into the building.

The day brought a mix of emotions for Max; on the one hand, every time her skirt rubbed against her skin, she was reminded of the spanking coming her way—but she also thought of naughty things. Things she had no business thinking about regarding one Rafe Jennings.

But she knew there was absolutely no point in pinning any fantasies on him. They would never come true.

Maxine needed to find a guy who was really attainable for someone like her, a guy who might not be the stuff of fantasies but would have real arms to hold her when the fantasies grew old and cold in her bed.

Which was probably why, when Max, sans panties, ran into Ted from the mailroom on her lunch and he asked her out, she said yes. Ted was not terribly attractive, but he was a real man and he was asking.

Maybe after dinner, she'd tell him she wasn't wearing any panties, Max thought rather daringly, then sighed, knowing she wouldn't.

Max arranged to meet Ted at 5:45 in front of the building; surely forty-five minutes was long enough to allot for a spanking. Lord, she hoped so, or dinner would be decidedly unpleasant!

• • • • • • •

Max took a deep breath and knocked on Rafe's office door.

"Come in," his deep voice came from the other side of the door.

She opened it and closed it behind her as she entered the lion's den.

"I'm glad to see you made it here on time today, Maxine."

"Like I had a choice," she muttered under her breath.

Rafe raised a brow as he walked to stand in front of her. "Still have a bit of an attitude, I see. I'd hoped the day without panties would help with that."

He took her arm firmly and led her to the corner. "Can't we just get this over with?" she asked.

Rafe's left brow shot up. "In a hurry? I think a little corner time with your bottom on display will help get you in a better frame of mind to deal with your discipline, young lady."

Max sighed loudly but allowed him to place her in the corner with her skirt rucked up around her waist. She stood there fidgeting and worrying how long all this would take. She glanced nervously over her shoulder at the clock on the wall.

"Somewhere pressing to be, Maxine?"

"I kind of have a date," she said softly, embarrassed to be discussing her love life while standing bare-bottomed in the corner with the man who planned to spank said bottom thoroughly.

"You have a what?" Rafe growled.

Max jumped, totally unprepared for the volatile reaction. She dropped her skirt and spun to face him, where he stood angrily a few feet behind her.

"A date," she whispered, almost afraid to say it out loud again.

"With another man?"

Max blinked. "Well… umm… we aren't…"

"The hell we aren't!"

Inexplicably, tears began to gather in her eyes. "But you never said we were anything and I didn't think the possibility even existed and Ted seemed nice enough and I didn't want to be alone anymore and… and…" To her horror Max was suddenly sobbing.

The anger seemed to drain from Rafe's face as he scooped her up and carried her with him back to his big desk chair where he sat cuddling her close as she sobbed into his chest. "Honey, I'm so sorry. I should have made myself clear. I always meant to claim you for my own."

Max sniffed and leaned back to glare up at him. "Claim me? That's a tad nineteenth century, don't you think!"

He grinned as he leaned down to kiss the tip of her very red nose. "I feel a tad nineteenth century when it comes to you, honey, and make no mistake, when I take you it will be a claiming. I plan to leave you in no doubt whatsoever who you belong to."

Even though heat filled her loins, Max was a bit affronted by the machismo oozing from his pores. "I belong to myself, Rafe Jennings!"

"Be fair, honey; if I'm going to belong to you, shouldn't you belong to me?" he asked with a fake pout.

Silly man! Max knew she'd just been caught hook, line, and sinker, chauvinist pig or not, but a tiny niggling doubt still tied her tummy in knots. Fixing her eyes on a shirt button, she softly asked, "You really want me that way?"

Rafe tilted her face up to his and showed her the quickest way he knew, by kissing her senseless. It took only seconds for Max to melt into him as his tongue stole into her mouth to duel with her own.

She sighed deeply, leaning forward for more when Rafe set her gently away from him, "You've been tying me in knots for months, Maxine."

"I have?" she asked breathlessly.

"You have," he grinned, before lifting her to stand in front of him and firmly meeting her gaze. "To the corner with you, young lady."

"The corner? But I thought…"

"That's exactly why I haven't started this conversation with you yet. I didn't want you to think it would get you out of a well-deserved spanking and I'm telling you right now, it won't… ever."

Max blinked up at him again. "Oh…"

"Yeah, oh!" he said with a firm swat to her bottom urging her back to the corner. "Get that bottom bare, young lady, and don't you move a muscle while I'm gone."

"Where are you going?" she asked from her position in the corner; suddenly it was a lot more bearable now that she knew he actually cared about her.

"I need to go tell our mailroom Casanova that you won't be free tonight or any other night."

Max took heart from the vehemence in his voice; he really, really wanted her.

• • • • • • •

Rafe was back in record time, leaving a brokenhearted Ted in his wake.

"Was Ted okay?" Max asked from her corner.

"He'll get over it. He can find his own girl; you belong to me," Rafe said before placing the straight-backed chair in the center of the room and calling her to him.

Max came quietly, placing herself across his thighs without hesitation.

"Why are we here, Maxine?"

"I've been reading at my desk instead of working," she answered honestly, eager to get this behind them.

"Are you ever going to do that again?" he asked as he ran one broad palm across her upturned bottom.

"No, sir," she said softly.

"Let's make sure," Rafe said, firmly tucking her in tight, his hand slapping down immediately. He spanked her hard and fast from the very beginning, leaving no room for doubt that this was a punishment spanking.

After the tenth swat, the intense sting and heat had quickly built in her bottom and Max gasped and started kicking.

Rafe left not an inch of skin free from his attention; he brought her bottom from pink to red and then from red to crimson, leaving her limp and sobbing across his lap before he stopped and brought her up to sit once again on his knee.

Max winced as her roasted bottom came in contact with his pants, finding it really difficult to sit there with tonight's spanking resting on top of the thorough spanking from last night.

Rafe cuddled her close and rubbed her back as she calmed. "That's my good girl. You took your punishment very well, baby, I'm proud of you."

Oddly enough, those words gave her a sense of pride. She could take a well-earned spanking like a woman. Like Rafe's woman.

## CHAPTER FIVE

Max didn't demure as Rafe followed her up the stairs to her apartment. She was over the moon, even with a flaming backside. Rafe Jennings wanted her! Would he make love to her tonight?

She sure hoped so... she'd waited forever for a man to come along who brought forth more than a lukewarm response.

Rafe stirred a virtual inferno to life within her veins and now she could explore it to her heart's content, as long as she played her cards right.

Max walked into her apartment and dithered around the entry way, out of her depth and unsure how to proceed with her plans to thoroughly seduce the big man. "Umm, would you like a cup of coffee or something? I can make dinner..."

Rafe leaned against a wall and stared at her intently, watching her where she stood playing nervously with the end of her scarf. He hadn't said anything since they left the parking garage and even then he'd only instructed her to fasten her seatbelt.

She sucked her lower lip between her teeth. Had she already done something to make him angry again?

As if he'd reached a decision, Rafe nodded and

straightened from the wall, walking toward her with intent written clearly in his eyes.

Max felt her eyes widen as she backed away from his advancing figure, suddenly panicked and unsure if seduction was a good plan. She didn't know what she was doing!

All the sex manuals and romances in the world did not really give one applicable knowledge of how to put anything into action. Surely it went beyond the mechanics? Would it be instinctual?

Her face heated as she kept backing across the room. Rafe continued to silently stalk her across the floor until her back came to rest against the wall between the living room and kitchen. The feel of the cool wall against her hot bottom through the thin material of her skirt reminded Max she still wasn't wearing any panties.

A throbbing heat sprang to life between her thighs and she felt her face flush anew, but this time it was with need.

Rafe still said nothing as he moved to cage her against the wall between his arms, his big body resting inches away from her own.

Max swallowed as she looked up into the eyes staring so intently into her own, her small tongue darting out to lick her suddenly dry lips.

His head swooped in to cover her trembling mouth with his own. It was a soft whisper of a kiss, the barest touch before he cupped her face gently in his hands and moved back a few inches to study her some more. "Are you ready, Maxine?"

"Ready?" she squeaked breathlessly, the tension between them palpable.

"Ready to become mine? Be sure because I warn you, once you give yourself to me, there will be no going back. I won't ever let you go."

She smiled up at him shyly. "Who said I wanted you to let me go?"

Then she was in his arms, pressed tightly against his hard body as he kissed her deeply and thoroughly. Max gasped as his big hands found their way beneath her skirt and cupped her tender bottom to lift her tight against his erection.

The hot sting in her bottom seemed to spread through her veins, wringing a soft moan from her lips. She wrapped her arms around his neck and instinctively brought her legs up and around his waist, suddenly wanting to be closer to him than it even seemed possible and whimpering when it wasn't enough.

"Shhh, baby, I've got you," he soothed her as he carried her into the bedroom and stood her in front of him as he began to unbutton her blouse.

Max couldn't be still; she pressed soft kisses against any bit of skin she could reach, hardly noticing the absence of her shirt or the skirt that quickly followed. Her hands skimmed beneath his shirt, trying to shove it up over his head as she felt her breasts fall free from her bra.

Rafe dropped to his knees in front of her, taking one pouty nipple into his mouth.

She shuddered, cradling his head to her breast as he sucked her deep. One hand held her to him as the other skimmed her round bottom, caressing and palming it before giving it a lightly stinging swat.

Max gave a soft mewl of shocked pleasure as he continued to rain swats across her bottom, reawakening the sting from earlier. All the while he continued to nibble and suck at first one nipple then the other, leaving Max awash in sensation. When his fingers skimmed once again across her bottom and then delved between her legs to seat one long finger deep inside, her knees buckled. Only the firm arm at her waist kept her upright.

"So hot and wet. Is this for me?" he asked.

She didn't answer, writhing against his invading finger, lost in the need building inside her. The delightful finger was gone and a much sharper smack fell on her unsuspecting bottom. Max gasped, her hips bucking in response.

"I asked you a question, young lady."

"Wh-what?" Max asked breathlessly. Her head fell back

on her shoulders as that wicked finger came back to play along her slick passage.

"I asked if this was for me."

"Yes… please…" She begged for something that seemed just out of her reach.

Rafe moved quickly to spill her backwards on the bed and hooked her legs over his shoulders, opening her fully to his gaze.

"Rafe?" she asked, suddenly unsure.

"So pretty, how could I resist a taste?"

Max didn't have time to decide if she wanted this or not, because before his intent had time to completely register, his mouth covered her, his tongue taking her masterfully.

She cried out and pressed her hips helplessly up to his marauding mouth, feeling like she would explode at any minute. When he circled her sensitive nub with his tongue as he pressed his thumb into her with a circular motion, she came with a scream of surprise, trying to pull away from the intensity of what she was feeling.

Rafe allowed no such retreat, holding her fast as he continued to work her with his talented tongue and fingers. Incredibly she began to build toward another orgasm immediately and when he sucked her between his lips she skyrocketed off again, yelling his name.

Max lay boneless with her legs hanging off the edge of the bed, panting for breath. Her eyes widened as Rafe stood and began to remove his own clothes. She blushed as she realized he'd been fully clothed while he'd brought her to completion twice.

When he peeled his pants and underwear from his body and his erection sprang forth, she eyed it with a little trepidation. It seemed huge, long, and thick. Max wondered if perhaps she should mention she'd never actually done this before. Suddenly everything she'd read seemed anatomically impossible.

"Rafe… I haven't exactly…"

He gave her such a look of tenderness it almost stole her

breath and chased away most of the uncertainty. "I know, baby, it'll be okay. Trust me?"

Max nodded, then looked pointedly at his erection. "What if it doesn't fit?"

He laughed and then came down over her, easily getting her caught up in their mutual desire again to take her mind off the mechanics involved.

She groaned, surprised how good it felt to have his weight come down over her, pressing her deep into the mattress. He began to nibble along her neck, making her shiver in response, his fingers coming between them to stroke her back into readiness. Soon she was writhing against him again, opening her legs in shameless invitation.

Rafe fitted himself to the opening of her body and stilled, looking down at her.

Max frowned and tried to move, but he held her fast. "Please," she moaned demandingly, her body clamoring for the satisfaction it knew he could provide.

"Look at me, Maxine." At his firm tone she opened her eyes and looked up into his.

As soon as she made eye contact he thrust home, seating himself to the hilt. Max felt uncomfortably full at first, but there was no real pain, and after a moment she was eager for more. But Rafe remained determinedly still.

She watched the play of emotions over Rafe's face as he waited for her to adjust to him. Her brow puckered in a frown and she tried to wriggle and force him into movement as he groaned. "Wait, Maxine, give yourself a minute..."

"I don't want a minute. I want you to move... now..." she said in sudden demand as she grabbed his face and pulled it down to her own to kiss him aggressively, sliding her tongue against his.

Rafe returned her kiss almost desperately as he began to move, riding her slowly, pulling out inch by inch almost all the way before sliding back into her just as slowly.

Max groaned and wrapped her legs around his hips, trying to bring him back more quickly, but Rafe was determined to set the pace. She wanted to scream as her need built and built but the same maddening rhythm continued, then when he pressed a finger lightly between them in just the right spot, she catapulted over the edge once again.

Then he started moving faster and harder, taking her deeper, as deep as her body would allow. Max met him thrust for thrust, enjoying the increasing strength of his movements. When he once again palmed her backside to help arch her into him, she exploded once again.

Then he began to pound into her, taking his own satisfaction, grinding against her with a groan as he came and bringing her with him yet again.

Max felt like a puddle of melted wax when he sank down onto the bed next to her and pulled her tight against him.

"That was... wow," she said softly, her hand playing lightly with the hair on his chest as she snuggled even closer.

Rafe laughed and kissed the top of her head. "I can live with wow. Just so long as you realize you now belong irrevocably to me."

Max kissed his chest. "Yep, and the same goes for you, buddy," she said with a yawn followed with a soft snore.

• • • • • • •

When Max woke, she wriggled her body experimentally against Rafe's larger frame; he merely snored louder and pulled her tighter against him in response.

She smiled, the satisfied smile of a woman well loved. Her body was deliciously sore in unexpected places and she could still feel the gentle thrum of her climaxes pulsing between her legs.

Rafe had done exactly as he'd promised her. His possession had been ruthlessly thorough, and even now in his sleep he clutched her tightly as if to prevent her escape.

His claim made her feel so complete, she almost felt branded. With a sigh, Max touched his cheek, softly wondering if it truly went both ways... knowing if it didn't she would be emotionally eviscerated.

Max wanted to believe in the happy ending as much as the next girl, to give herself completely... trusting Rafe was the real deal, but did it have to feel like jumping off a skyscraper without a safety net?

# CHAPTER SIX

Max floated on air the next day at work and soared through the skies with Rafe as her guide the next night. He made love to her throughout the night, not letting her fall into an exhausted slumber until it was almost dawn.

She was amazed by the energy pulsing through her body when she got up for work even with so little sleep. Max grinned saucily up at Rafe as she passed him on her way out of the bathroom. "They should bottle you and send you out for mass marketing! That morning drag getting you down? Who needs energy drinks? Just take a Rafe all night long and you'll be in fighting form when you wake ready to face the day!"

Rafe growled under his breath, giving her a light slap on the bottom to propel her out the bathroom door.

Max turned in the doorway with a pretend look of surprise. "Feeling under the weather, sugar? I guess I wore you out, perhaps we should get you some vitamins or you should eat some Wheaties... noooo!"

Max screamed with laughter as he suddenly tossed her over his shoulder, tickling her all the way to the bed, where he dropped her unceremoniously with mock sternness. "Get ready for work, young woman. None of this tomfoolery!"

"Spoilsport!" she yelled as he went back into the bathroom to take his own shower.

Max sighed wistfully. If he weren't such a stickler for being on time, she would join him in the shower and... "Uh-oh... two nights and I'm a nympho!"

Laughing to herself, Max finished getting ready for work. She decided she didn't care if she was a nympho; no woman would with Rafe Jennings in her bed.

• • • • • • •

Max was humming to herself when Rafe buzzed her on the intercom. "Maxine, meet me at the truck. We're going to lunch."

"Okay," she said with a grin and barely managed to keep from leaping from her desk in full song. *I feel pretty... I feel pretty... see the pretty girl in that mirror there... What mirror where...*

"Max, did you finish the report on Cummings Diesel?"

She jumped; thank goodness she hadn't been singing out loud! "Hi, Bob! Here it is, see you later, I have a hot date!" Max grinned at him after handing over the report and grabbing her purse. "See ya after lunch!"

Rafe was already sitting in the driver's seat when Max climbed in next to him. She frowned; he didn't turn to her with a kiss or even a smile.

"Is something wrong?"

"We'll talk about it over lunch."

Max felt her heart drop into her shoes. He was going to break up with her! She spent the rest of the drive staring morosely out the window. Stupid jerk! He should never have made her fall in love with him. She should have stuck with Ted from the mailroom, someone she could manage.

Rafe pulled into a parking spot at Cracker Barrel; Max just turned to him with a glare. "I don't feel like eating."

"Tough," he said succinctly as he got out of the car. She

watched him walk around to her side and open the door. Max just looked at him.

"I'd rather not."

"Come along, Maxine, we have things to discuss," Rafe said firmly, taking her arm to pull her from the truck and then after him into the restaurant.

"Quit pulling, I'm coming! Under duress but I'm coming," Max muttered sourly.

Rafe leaned down to whisper in her ear, "You're in enough trouble, young lady, don't make it worse."

She blinked; in trouble? What did she do now? Part of her was relieved, maybe he didn't want to break up, but the other part was indignant he felt he had the right to take her to task over anything.

It wasn't crowded yet so they were seated quickly. Max frowned again when Rafe immediately handed the menus back to the server. "We'll both just have the chicken salad sandwich with chips and a glass of sweet tea."

"What if I didn't want chicken salad?" Max asked in outrage.

"You always order chicken salad when we get food here. Stop looking for an argument," he said firmly.

Part of her was flattered he remembered her preference, but Max wasn't ready to climb down off her high horse yet. "Maybe I didn't want chicken salad today."

"Enough, Maxine," he said flatly. "I had an interesting conversation with the mechanic working on your car today."

Max brightened. "Is it ready?"

"Yes, but that's not why he called. He wanted to know if you wanted your glasses." Rafe's voice rose a bit as he pulled her orange glasses case with a Yorkie puppy on it from his pocket and plunked it down on the table between them.

She winced and gave a nervous laugh. "You don't say?"

"Maxine."

"It's not that big of a deal," Max said with a frown.

"You can't mess with your eyes, Maxine. If you need glasses, you should be wearing them. I can't remember ever seeing you in a pair of glasses so you obviously aren't taking care of your eyes."

Max deflated the beginnings of a pout forming on her face. "I don't really need them that bad."

"They're bifocals!" Rafe said loudly.

Max and the waitress who was bringing their food both jumped.

"Really, Rafe, is it necessary to yell? Besides, they're ugly!" she snapped back at him in exasperation.

Rafe took a deep breath before turning to the waitress. "Could you bag that up to go, please?"

Max felt her bottom cheeks clench; perhaps contrite would have been a better approach. "Rafe, I know I should have…"

"Too late."

"But…"

"Save it," he said with a glare.

"I'm going to the ladies' room," she said with a disdainful sniff.

"Fine. I'll meet you at the cash register. It'll give me time to browse."

Max rolled her eyes as she walked through the country store in the lobby on her way to the restroom. The man had all but told the entire dining room he was going to bust her butt and now he was browsing? The whole situation was preposterous!

It wasn't like she was used to answering to anyone. She'd ignored her need for glasses long before they were dating. Long before he'd ever spanked her. It wasn't fair for him to bring up past failings. While Max recognized this particular past failing was also a current one, it wasn't as if she'd been able to take care of it. After all, her car was in the shop and the glasses had been in the car.

Deciding this was the approach to take, Max headed out to meet Rafe at the register, and promptly froze when she saw what he was handing to the clerk behind the counter.

It was a paddle ball! Max was mortified. She looked nervously at the clerk. "That's not for me... it's for my nephew... he collects paddles... I mean paddle balls... he really likes the game!" Max knew the red heat climbing into her face was totally belying her words.

Rafe snorted as he paid the suddenly tongue-tied clerk, who was blushing almost as much as Max. "Have a nice day." she said rather weakly to Max before she turned to follow Rafe's determined stride out the door.

"I can't believe you did that to me!" Max yelled as she climbed into the truck.

"I didn't do anything, Maxine, you were the one who gave the game away and I refuse to take any responsibility for the scene you just played out in there," Rafe said firmly.

"I will never eat at Cracker Barrel again," she exclaimed.

Rafe just grunted and continued to drive. Max frowned as she realized they were driving back to her apartment. "I have to go back to work!"

"No, you don't. I called while you were in the bathroom and said you weren't feeling well."

"I feel fine!" she squeaked.

"You won't by the time I'm finished with you," Rafe said matter-of-factly.

Max gulped and stared at the sack sitting innocuously on top of the dash with morbid fascination.

"I've learned my lesson!"

He just snorted in disbelief.

"It's not fair. We weren't dating when I stopped wearing my glasses and since we started dating, my car's been in the shop with my glasses! Isn't there some sort of grandfather clause that says you can't spank me for things in the past?"

"I'm using the grandfather clause that states I can spank you if the thing in the past is still of an outstanding nature."

"But my car is in the shop and my glasses have been in the car!"

"Why is your car in the shop?" he asked as if curious.

"Because I hit you, but that's beside the point!"

"Actually, Maxine, that is exactly the point; all of the past two weeks are an example of you behaving in an irresponsible manner. All you had to do was say you needed your glasses from the car, but you chose not to do so. It's all tied together and I think we need to nip this rebellious irresponsibility in the bud."

"Consider it nipped!" she squawked as he parked in front of her building.

"It's about to be well and truly nipped," he said resolutely.

This time Max practically raced him to her door; maybe if she got there before him she could... no such luck. Silly long-legged man!

"Corner."

"Don't you want to talk about this?"

"I think everything's been pretty much said. Corner. One..."

"Fine!" Max yelled as she stomped to the corner, where she stood fidgeting from one foot to the other. He had a paddle... how bad was it going to be... worse than his hand? As bad as the belt?

Rafe set the sandwich plates down on the counter before sitting down on the couch with his other purchase. She watched out of the corner of her eye as he painstakingly pulled the large staple holding the rubber string and ball out of the lightweight paddle. It was smaller than the ones from the grocery store, more compact but a tad thicker. All in all it was sturdy little fly-back paddle. She shuddered when he swished it in the air experimentally and grinned, apparently satisfied it would serve his purposes.

"Come here, Maxine," he ordered.

Max stayed in the corner, her nose pressed tightly into it. "I'm still reflecting on the error of my ways."

"Now, Maxine."

Her shoulders slumped in defeat before Max turned to face him and walked slowly to her doom. *Stupid paddle...*

*stupid scary paddle...*

When she was standing before him, Rafe wasted no time pulling her down across his thighs and baring her bottom to his gaze and to the paddle.

He didn't take any time for a warm-up but just got to business bringing the little paddle down with a loud crack that seemed to echo around the living room.

Max yowled as the sting filled her backside with fire, barely having time to absorb it before the paddle fell a second time and then a third. She quickly lost count as it fell again and again rapidly across her writhing bottom.

Rafe kept up a quick and steady rhythm, watching as he painted her bottom several shades of red then an intriguing shade of scarlet.

Max hung limply over his knee feeling as if her bottom would explode into flames any minute and set the wicked little paddle on fire. She would not mourn its demise.

A shuddering sigh of relief ran through her as Rafe stopped for a moment, then she realized he was only tipping her further over so he could pay special attention to the spot where her thighs and bottom met and she started crying anew.

Rafe blazed another path of glory across the sweet spot now opened up to him and continued to paddle her as if he would never stop.

Max suddenly felt as if something cracked open inside her and released every bit of tension held within her body in a mighty sigh of surrender, letting go of her last bit of control. She sobbed loudly, not even registering the spanking had stopped. She gave him everything that was within her and with the release came freedom and blessed peace.

Rafe loved her; no matter how far up the cliff was, he would catch her... Rafe was her net. When she lost control, he would be there to bring her back in focus, he would give her clarity.

He would love her. She was his and he was hers.

## CHAPTER SEVEN

The next morning Max awoke to Rafe handing her the little red cell phone she'd so desperately missed and her car keys.

He seemed distant and not at all like the man who'd held her in his arms during the night.

"I don't understand. I thought you said I couldn't have my car for…"

"Something's come up, my old boss called this morning and I'm needed in Washington for a few weeks. I think you've learned your lesson. I'll drop you at work and then someone will deliver your car before you get off for the day," he explained.

"What about… well, I mean… I…" She sniffled as her eyes began to fill without her permission.

"Don't, Maxine," Rafe said softly, pulling her gently into his chest as he stroked a hand down her back. "I'll be back, I promise."

Then he kissed her gently and dropped her off at work.

• • • • • • •

She was able to convince herself he was coming back for

the first month. By the end of the second month she began to doubt everything they'd shared. Sure, he'd managed to call a few times, but the calls were short and the conversation stilted. There was the distance between them, and there was the worry about his safety, and then there was the strangeness of his calls, and soon Max began to have doubts. She wasn't sure she could handle it if he got hurt or even killed. It would be easier if he'd just been a fling. Then she could be angry, rather than worried. When each phone call was more and more stilted and magnified the distance between them, she realized it wasn't better at all; she missed him. After the third month passed, she decided it was all a lie; nothing had been real. Rafe had just wanted sex and the added kink of smacking her bottom.

Max had handed herself to him on a silver platter when she rear-ended him with a phone screen full of spanking stories. She'd made it so easy.

She was determined to never be such an easy mark for any man again. Max began to drop weight at an alarming rate; she had a hard time eating since her appetite was non-existent.

Rafe had talked about how beautiful her strawberry blond locks were, so Max cut them short and dyed her hair black. She began going out with some girls from work to happy hour and quickly found solace in vodka and losing herself on the dance floor.

Oddly now that she was almost too thin, men came at her in droves. She wasn't interested in anything but dancing and drinking as she tried to forget.

Max took to wearing kohl around her eyes, making them look like big cat eyes, stark in her pale face fringed by short black curls. Her glasses were a thing of the past; since the last spanking from Rafe about her glasses, Max had had Crystal Lens surgery to correct her vision.

Her breasts were still large looking, somewhat out of balance on her new thin frame.

・・・・・・・

When Rafe had been gone about four months, Tom, her boss, tried to talk with her about Rafe. "Max, I'm worried about you. You're far too thin and I know Rafe would…"

Max froze then looked up at him with a frown. "Rafe? I'm not sure what he has to do with anything, Tom. He doesn't work here anymore."

"Rafe will be back, Max," Tom said firmly.

"I'm sure that has nothing to do with me," Max said resolutely. "I need to finish these reports before I leave for the day, so if there is nothing else?"

She pointedly stared at the wall over his left shoulder until Tom sighed and left with a short goodbye.

・・・・・・・

Rafe was finally back in Washington; he'd been imbedded deep in the deserts of Iraq and Syria for the last five months on a black op pinpointing small ISIS cells so a crew could come in and clean out each nest.

He'd only agreed to the op for a few weeks until the man he was filling in for came back after the birth of his first child. The problem was after the birth of his child, the man no longer wished to participate in black ops.

It took Rafe the next four months to convince his superiors that he now had a reason to come home as well. He no longer felt like risking his own life so cavalierly. He'd done his part and parcel for his country. Now he wanted to spend the rest of his life loving his woman. Loving Maxine.

The first chance he got he called her, eager to tell her he was coming home; he closed his eyes when Max answered the phone. Hearing her sweet voice was enough to bring tears to his eyes.

"Hello, Maxine," he said softly. Silence greeted his words. "Max? It's Rafe."

"I know who it is, I just have no idea why you would be

calling me," Max said harshly.

"I told you I'd be back, Maxine," Rafe said firmly.

"You said you'd be back in a few weeks, but of course that was a lie just like everything else. I don't know why you're bothering to call me, Rafe. You won't find me easy pickings this time," Max said coldly.

"Nothing between us was a lie, Maxine," Rafe told her.

"Whatever, Rafe. I really don't have time to talk. I'm due to meet some friends at the club. Don't call again."

"Maxine, don't you dare…" He stopped when he realized he was talking to a dial tone. The little minx had hung up on him! Everything between them a lie indeed; he wondered how much of a lie she'd think it was next time he was blistering her backside.

Rafe told her when she gave herself to him that it was forever and she should have heeded his words, because he was home and he was going to reclaim everything that was his.

• • • • • • •

Max was reeling; why had he called now? Just when she was finally starting to feel normal again?

She put him determinedly from her mind; perhaps it was time to sleep with one of the guys at the club. Many had made a play for her attentions; the problem was none of them stirred her.

Not the way he did; even now just from the sound of his voice, her traitorous body was coming back to life. Every nerve was pulsing with an answering throb between her legs as the telling moisture began to seep from her core where she ached for his possession.

Max glared at her reflection in the mirror. No way was she going there again. The satisfaction he'd give her would be short-lived and the pain when he dumped her again would be something she might not recover from a second time.

Nope, Rafe was better left to memory... memories she could pull out in the dark of night and use her vibrator to assuage the yearnings of her body.

She studied her reflection once more before leaving for the club; the mermaid hair dye she'd used gave her an odd but striking look. Gone were the black tresses she'd sported for the previous few months; now her hair hung around her shoulders bleeding from purple on the crown of her head to a brilliant blue then finally to the turquoise that swung freely around her shoulders.

Max shrugged; she wasn't entirely sure she liked it but it would do for now. One thing she'd really enjoyed in the last several months was continually reinventing herself. The weight hadn't really been deliberate. She'd just lost her appetite for anything except the blessed relief the vodka gave her. When she was drunk and muzzy-headed, she was able to laugh and dance and for a little while forget all about Rafe Jennings.

Before Rafe she'd never really drank, she was really quite the goody-goody. But after he left, in an effort to pull her from her dark depression, her coworker Sally had finally convinced her to try happy hour.

After the first few drinks, Max had discovered peace from her busy thoughts of Rafe and whatever she did to drive him away. Blessed silence in her meandering mind... suddenly she was able to live in the moment and to her surprise the alcohol also served to get past the natural reserve and shyness she'd always experienced in social situations.

Now Max could interact with everyone else with ease once she'd had a drink and the dancing; she loved to dance and lose herself in the music swirling around her in the dark heat of the night.

Suddenly Max was almost desperate to escape the silence in her apartment; she would forget her problems minutes after walking into the club... she would give herself up to the fuzzy-headed peace the alcohol provided and then lose herself in the dance. Maybe tonight she'd find a man who could help her forget Rafe's touch.

# CHAPTER EIGHT

Rafe followed Tom into the dimly lit club with a frown. Max was here? This wasn't the type of place Maxine frequented. The air was filled with desperation... desperate people looking for something, anything to fill the empty void of their lives.

Max was vibrant and alive, she didn't belong here; this place would suck the life out of her and leave her a hard shell.

"Are you sure Maxine will be here?" he asked dubiously.

Tom looked at him with a little sadness in his eyes. "Max is here every night, Rafe. I told you she's different. Harder... at least on the surface; she never smiles anymore. I'm not sure you'll even recognize her."

Rafe frowned finding it hard to reconcile what Tom was saying with his Maxine. Then Tom pointed out the small figure moving her body seductively on the dance floor. He froze with shock; the strawberry waves that used to fall down her back were gone. Instead her hair hung about shoulder length and was an odd mix of purples and blues and she was scarily thin. The curves he'd enjoyed so much were now just hard angles with the exception of her breasts; they were still enticingly full but looked out of place on her almost emaciated frame.

He watched as she danced; she barely even seemed to be aware of her partner as she moved to the beat. The man she was dancing with didn't care, he used every opportunity he could to brush his body against hers in a sick parody of making love.

Rafe found himself getting angry; what the hell was she thinking letting some strange man rub himself around on her like that? Her behavior was beyond risky.

Before he even knew what he was doing, Rafe was standing in front of her on the dance floor, Romeo shoved roughly to one side.

Maxine didn't even seem to notice her partner had changed at first, she was so caught up in the music, but when he took a firm hold of her waist and jerked her pliant body against his own, she stiffened and her eyes flew open in alarm.

He watched as her alcohol-muddled brain tried to make sense of being in his arms; it took a minute but soon she was trying to jerk away. "Let me go, Rafe."

Ignoring the angry little demand, he pulled her closer and began to slow dance around the floor despite the fast beat thrumming around them.

She felt so good in his arms, even with the hard little bones poking him when before he'd felt only soft womanly curves. One of his first orders of business would be to put some weight back on his woman.

"I've missed you, Maxine," he said softly into the shell of her ear and was rewarded with a soft shuddering sigh before she stomped hard on his instep.

"Let me go, you big ass!" Max yelled up at him.

He grunted at the slight pain in his foot and loosened his hold a little but didn't release her. "I'll let that one slide, baby. We've got to talk. You've got it all wrong…"

Maxine reared her hand back and slapped him solidly across the face, the anger behind the blow enough to give her the strength to make his ears ring.

When she started to lift the other hand, he caught her wrist before it could connect. "Tread very carefully."

She glared up at him before finally dropping her gaze from his. "Fine, will you please let go of my arm? I don't feel well and would like to go home."

"Okay, I'll give you a ride," he told her and began to lead her off the dance floor, ignoring all the very interested stares their exchange had garnered.

"I can take myself," she spat.

"Not in your current condition you can't, young lady. You're drunk and I better not find out you drive yourself around regularly in this condition," he said sternly.

"Whether I do or not is no business of yours, Rafe Jennings!" Max practically screamed, demonstrating just how drunk she was.

"That's enough," Rafe said, turning her to face him firmly. "You have two choices. You can walk out of here on your own steam or you can ride out over my shoulder. Which is it going to be, Max?"

"Pig!" she yelled as she kicked him neatly in the shin.

"Shoulder it is," Rafe said as calmly as he could, given he wanted to toss her over a knee and paddle the tar out of her. He managed not to, instead tossing her lightly over his right shoulder and taking her purse from Tom.

"See you at the office tomorrow," Tom called after him as he walked out of the club with an irate Maxine yelling curse words and pounding his back from her position over his shoulder.

Rafe delivered one sharp swat to her bottom. "That's enough!" Her struggles stopped, immediately reminding him how beautifully she'd responded to his discipline.

He sat her firmly in the seat of his truck and buckled her in, which garnered him another glare. "We'll talk more at your apartment."

Max made the ride home in complete silence; he could see the rage building in her as she worked herself up. He watched the rapid play of emotions across her face with concern but she continued to ignore him. As if it was no business of his how she felt and she resented his interference.

When the truck stopped in front of her apartment, Max jumped out and ran inside.

"Maxine, wait!" he called after her and cursed when she ignored him. Rafe walked into the apartment building, doing a quick perimeter check then a walk through before finding her in the kitchen pouring herself yet another drink. Rafe frowned; it was clear Maxine was drinking way too much. "What the hell are you playing at, Maxine? You know better than to just run in like that."

"Leave me alone, Rafe. I'm tired and I needed a drink," she said, pouring a generous amount of vodka in her glass.

Rafe frowned at her. "That won't help, Maxine," he said in a gentle voice.

She suddenly whirled on him in a fury. "Don't you dare presume to tell me what I do and do not need, Rafe Jennings!" Max yelled before flinging the glass and its contents at him.

He ducked and the glass shattered on the floor behind him.

They stood staring across the kitchen at each other.

"You have no idea what I need," she said, her voice raw.

"What do you need, baby?" Rafe asked.

Max suddenly gave him a brittle smile and started toward him. "Do you really want to help me?"

"Of course I do, honey, just tell me what you need," he said.

Max started unzipping his pants the minute she reached him. Rafe caught her hand, shocked by her boldness. She laughed and jerked her hand away. "This is what I need but I can find it someplace else."

She snatched her purse off the counter and walked out of the kitchen.

He grabbed her before she made it to the front door, swinging her around to face him. Max's purse fell to the floor and she slapped him hard across the face.

Rafe caught her wrist and pulled her close. "Feel better?"

She looked at the quickly reddening handprint on his cheek and smiled. "Yeah…" she said just before his mouth came down hard on hers.

It wasn't a gentle kiss but it fit the mood. Maxine ground her mouth hard against his and wrapped her arms tightly around him. He lifted her with his hands beneath her bottom and brought her tightly against him. She groaned and hooked her legs around him. Rafe sat her on the back of the couch and reached a hand between their bodies. As his hand grasped the crotch of her panties, he paused and looked down at her.

"You sure this is what you want?" he asked hoarsely.

In answer she unzipped his pants and freed him. "Just shut up and do it," Maxine said, nipping him sharply on the chin.

Rafe ripped her panties off and surged into her waiting heat. He groaned and reached to pull her chest against his, but Max put a hand against his chest and laid back across the couch, her legs around his thighs, so that where his body joined hers was the only place they touched.

He frowned but grabbed her bottom tightly to hold her steady as he began to pound into her, giving her what she seemed to think she needed. It was hard and fast, only taking a matter of moments for Max to stiffen beneath him and cry out as she began to convulse around him. Rafe followed her quickly and rested his head on her chest in the aftermath.

He raised his head at the sudden sob that wracked her body.

Max's eyes filled with tears and she pressed her hand against her mouth as if to stop the sobs. She shoved at Rafe roughly, as if horrified by what she'd just done. Rafe immediately let her up.

"Maxine," he said, reaching out a hand.

She put a hand up to ward him off, then ran into the bathroom, slamming the door. Why had she done that? She knew better to think she could use Rafe for a quick lay without major repercussions. There was nothing easy or simple about the feelings he roused in her.

Max looked into the mirror and stiffened her chin. She would not cry. Running cold water into the sink, she splashed it across her face until she was back in control of herself.

Max opened the bathroom door to find Rafe standing there waiting; she straightened her back and did her best to look through him.

He reached a hand out and gently stroked her cheek. "Max..."

Max batted his hands away as he pulled her close to his chest. "Stop it! Don't!" she screamed, fighting him as he wrapped his arms around her and began to stroke her back.

"It's okay to cry, baby," he said softly.

"Shut up!" Max yelled as she began beating on his chest. He held her fast and she suddenly collapsed against him with a broken sob. The tight rein she'd kept on herself and her tough façade was shattered by his gentleness. Great heaving sobs shook her body.

Rafe sank to the floor and pulled her into his lap, simply rocking and holding her while she sobbed out both her hurt and her unresolved feelings about his return. He continued stroking her back and murmuring soothing words while she quieted.

"Why'd you have to come back?" she asked almost fearfully against his neck.

Rafe froze for a minute and then resumed stroking her and said matter-of-factly, "I came back for you, Maxine, and I'm going to reclaim everything that belongs to me, baby girl. You're just going to have to learn to forgive me."

Another deep shuddering sob shook her frame. "I can't.

I won't."

"Yes, you will, baby girl. You don't have a choice. You love me as much as I love you," he said, shushing her when she would have protested.

Max let herself relax in to him for a moment; resting her head against him felt so right, but she knew better and she wouldn't let him do this to her a second time. Firming her resolve, she stiffened her back, pushed out of his arms, and got to her feet.

"I want you to leave," she said quietly but firmly.

"Maxine..." Rafe reached to catch hold of her again.

"No!" Max looked up and straight into his eyes. "I can't talk about this anymore tonight. I need some space."

She watched him struggle with his decision, but finally he nodded and she breathed a sigh of relief.

"I'll go for now, Maxine, but this is far from over."

Max had mixed feelings when the door closed behind him. Perversely there was a part of her that wished he'd argued to stay.

Shaking her head, she poured herself a healthy shot of vodka, ignoring the sharp pain in her stomach when it hit. Soon the blessed relief of fuzziness would fog her worry-torn mind and she'd be able to sleep.

# CHAPTER NINE

Maxine studied the information on the screen while worrying her lower lip with her teeth. Could she really go through with this?

Eight hundred dollars was a lot of money and would just about completely deplete her savings account, but another man was just what she needed to make Rafe think they were done. Too bad she had to pay for him, but then again, an escort made parting again much less messy. There was no chance the guy would think she was harboring feelings and she didn't have to put too much effort into being nice since she was paying.

She booked Javier for the night, having already decided that hiring him for the whole night was necessary to ensure the proper message was delivered. It had been tempting to just part with four hundred for three hours but at that hourly rate the full-night fee was a steal and really what she needed. It wasn't like she had to actually have sex with the guy, unless of course she wanted to and then she would.

Maybe she should; a good lay by an expert would surely drive all thoughts of Rafe Jennings and his sexual prowess right out of her mind. She had a while to decide; Javier wouldn't pick her up till seven. Hopefully he would live up to his write-up and the pictures on the Dallas Escorts site.

He was certainly gorgeous, tall with wonderfully broad shoulders and dark Latin good looks and his photos exuded a level of experience that should definitely give Rafe pause.

She'd given instructions to the service that Javier was to greet her like they had an ongoing relationship rather than meeting for the first time. Max just hoped he was able to be convincing.

• • • • • • •

Rafe pulled up in front of Maxine's apartment building geared for battle. As far as he was concerned, their reconciliation was a done deal. The fact that she'd tried to hold herself back was irrelevant because she hadn't been able to; she'd given herself into his keeping lock, stock, and barrel once again.

He stopped at the sight of a strange man standing at Maxine's door, and his jaw tightened when she opened the door and was swept into the man's arms for a penetrating kiss.

"I've missed you, Javier," she said in a throaty voice that made his blood boil.

"And I you, my lovely Max." The man's deep voice held a rhythmic accent that he obviously used in his favor when seducing women. "I've made a reservation for us at 560; I thought you'd enjoy the night view of the skyline while we became reacquainted."

Rafe frowned; 560 was the restaurant at the top of Reunion Tower that revolved in a complete circle over the course of an hour, giving its diners every possible view of the Dallas skyline. The name had been changed to 560 when Wolfgang Puck took it over; there had been a contest to rename the restaurant and 560 had won, since the restaurant stood 560 feet above the city. It was a place a man took a woman he wanted to impress.

"That sounds wonderful, Javie," she said, smiling up at

the guy from under her lashes.

Rafe glared; with her purple, blue, and turquoise hair waving about her shoulders, she looked all of sixteen instead of the twenty-eight years he knew her to be. What was this guy playing at? What was Maxine playing at? There was something familiar about the man, but he was too far away to get a good look at his face.

He took a deep breath, willing himself to calm down and see how the evening played out. Following them covertly would be child's play for him and would give him a better understanding of exactly what he was dealing with; something about the whole situation didn't quite ring true, once he pushed back the jealousy that came immediately roaring to the surface.

It was a waiting game right now and waiting out prey until they made a mistake was something Rafe excelled at; he'd bide his time and then spring at the perfect moment. Once he'd done so, it would take very little effort to make it clear to both Maxine and Javier who she belonged to and then he'd paddle her little ass for putting him to the trouble.

At this point he was unsure if he'd need to pound the mysterious Javier into the ground, but he definitely hoped it was on the books.

He frowned again as the couple came down the walk and Maxine rubbed a hand absently against her left side as if she was in pain. She'd done that a few times last night as well. Something else he would need to look into as she was obviously doing a piss-poor job of taking care of herself.

All in all, he had some work to do with Miss Maxine but she was worth it; he smiled as he remembered the sweet submission she'd given him before he'd left. He'd have that from her again and more. He'd have everything and he'd give her everything in return.

She just had to trust him again, but she would because Rafe wouldn't accept anything less. They'd have it all and live happily ever after.

He shook himself from his musings and visions of her

naked body draped over his lap for a long overdue lesson in behavior and hurried to his car. It would be best if he made it to the restaurant before them; then he could unobtrusively observe them from a good vantage point.

• • • • • • •

Max smiled at Javier. He was everything his write-up had claimed and more, but somehow everything about him left her cold.

All Rafe had to do was smile and or even slightly quirk a brow to start the pulse between her thighs throbbing double time and wetness to seep into the gusset of her panties. There was nothing Javier could do to elicit that sort of response from her. Over dinner as she and Javier chatted about inconsequential things, it was all Max could do to focus on the conversation at hand.

Her mind was filled with Rafe and how tender and understanding he'd been the night before and how horrid she'd been. Did he really deserve her scorn? He'd told her he was working for the government in the Middle East, though he couldn't disclose exactly where and she knew whatever he'd been doing was very important.

Everything between them had just been so new and the thought of losing him to foreign policy was more than she could deal with; Max wasn't sure she could handle a lifetime of not knowing where he was and being unsure if he'd come back to her whole or at all.

Rafe had called her three times during his long absence; the third call she hadn't answered because at that point she'd convinced herself everything they'd shared had been a lie. Then he'd sent Tom to try to talk to her in his stead and she'd shut Tom down before anything real could be communicated.

Max had a feeling she might have made the biggest mistake of her life by sending Rafe away the night before; an error that had now been compounded by Javier. The truth was she loved Rafe and needed him more than she wanted to admit to him or anyone else. Needing someone that much when they weren't available had caused her to make some rash choices. She'd been scared by how great her need for him was and had decided to cut him out of her life.

Then she'd started drinking to numb herself to the aching emptiness inside her; what if she was too late now? What if Rafe decided she wasn't worth the trouble? She'd been so drunk the night before, her memory was a little muzzy on what'd he'd told her; she knew they'd had sex... a flush stole up her cheeks as she remembered the blatant way she'd used him for sex. Rafe hadn't been happy with the situation, but he'd allowed it.

The fact that he had was telling in itself; before he'd left, Rafe would have simply paddled the daylights out of her, then taken her to bed and loved her so thoroughly she would have forgotten all her misgivings.

Max shook her head as she realized there was a fairly large part of her that wished he'd done exactly that... taken the choice and the control away from her. Then she wouldn't have to worry about making the right decision.

What a coward she was!

"My lovely Maxine, you are miles away from here, I think," Javier said softly in his cultured voice.

Max blinked and looked over into his understanding eyes. "I'm being terribly rude, please accept my apologies."

"No need to apologize, dear lady. I only hope he's worth all the thoughts flitting behind those lovely eyes," Javier said smoothly.

"Who?" she asked, trying to dismiss the knowing look in her escort's eyes.

Javier laughed. "The man who's been glaring daggers at me from the bar, I assume."

Max stiffened and looked over her shoulder and straight into Rafe's smoldering gaze, and everything below her waist clenched in response—her bottom winced in trepidation but everything else tensing in remembered pleasure. He was angry.

"Maybe we should go?" Max asked Javier hesitantly. They'd been lingering over coffee, but the air was thick with tension and no way did she want a confrontation with Rafe at the top of Reunion Tower.

"But of course, my dear, I aim only to please," he said with a grin, rising from the table and offering his hand. "Let's go; the check has already been paid."

Max sighed with relief as he led her quickly from the restaurant; they rode down in the glass elevator in complete silence, the view around them unseen.

Without a word Javier helped her into his low-slung Porsche and then drove quickly to her apartment.

"I give it about ten minutes before your man arrives to claim you," Javier said jovially as he walked her up to her apartment.

"Don't be silly…" Max began, only to be cut off by Rafe's terse voice.

"Less than that and you have about two seconds to tell me exactly what you're doing here." He stood with his back to the wall, facing Javier menacingly.

"Rafe, you've no right to…"

Rafe grabbed her arm firmly and pulled her to his side after liberating the keys from her suddenly lifeless fingers and opening the door. "I would be very careful how you talk to me right now, Maxine. You go on in your apartment while I deal with your friend. I expect to find you bare-bottomed and standing in the corner when I get inside."

"How dare you!" she gasped, embarrassed he'd spoken to her that way in front of Javier.

He simply delivered four sharp swats to her skirt-covered behind and pushed her gently into the door. "You're about to find out I'll dare a lot when it comes to you. Mind me now unless you want a spanking out here in the hall in front of this gentleman and the neighbors."

Max promptly closed her mouth and hurried inside,

pulling the door shut behind her with a satisfying bang.

∙ ∙ ∙ ∙ ∙ ∙ ∙

Rafe studied the man in front of him curiously; the man didn't seem to care that his romantic evening had been interrupted. Rafe had recognized Javier in the restaurant and would find out exactly what he was doing there now that Maxine was inside.

"I see now why the fair Maxine hired me, she was trying to get your attention," the man said with a smile.

Rafe frowned. "Hired you?"

"Yes, allow me to introduce myself, Javier Degrazio. Escort to lonely women in this fair city. Your Maxine paid for the whole night." The man's eyes twinkled with obvious amusement.

He growled under his breath, "Trying to get my attention, you think? I think she was trying to divert it."

"No, my friend, I assure you she wants it. She is conflicted at the moment, I think, but the way her eyes lit up when she saw you at the bar was unmistakable," the other man assured him.

Rafe sighed. "How much did she shell out for your services?"

"Eight hundred dollars; I was running a special. Usually my fees are higher," Degrazio said with a grin.

"Escorts have sales?" Rafe asked in disbelief; never in a million years would he have thought to be having this conversation with a fake gigolo on his woman's front doorstep. "Cut the fake smarmy accent, Jake."

The man in question snorted. "We were just trying to cover your back, commander."

"How did you come to know Maxine was looking for an escort?"

"Come on, Rafe, you know it's standard procedure to monitor Internet and phone activity on close friends and family when someone is planted deep. Especially new relationships," Jake replied.

"Of course, but I've been stateside for two weeks," Rafe said with a frown.

Jake shrugged. "We hadn't pulled the Internet surveillance yet and when your ladylove seemed to be trolling for company, we thought we'd better make sure she didn't end up with the real deal. I knew you'd been having some trouble and needed time to settle her back in."

Rafe closed his eyes and shook his head. His whole team knew Maxine had tried to hire a prostitute; he would never live this one down. "I'm going to paddle her backside raw."

Jake chuckled. "As it should be. If I had a woman and she dared to hire a man such as myself, I think she would not sit comfortably for quite some time. I know you have things to attend to so I will bid you goodnight."

He watched the man walk away and then considered Maxine's front door thoughtfully; this was going to require a little more of an impression than his hand could deliver and he was pretty sure the paddle he'd bought before going out of town was history. Good thing he had reinforcements in his truck.

A few minutes later when Rafe walked in Maxine's door with a small bag in his hand, she was standing not far away next to the couch.

"Is that the corner, young lady?"

Her spine stiffened and she glared up at him. "I will not be sent to the corner like some naughty child, Rafe Jennings! I'm an adult. If I want to entertain another man, I will do so!"

"I thought he was paid to entertain you. Did I misunderstand him when he was explaining you paid him eight hundred bucks for the night?"

Maxine gasped. "He told you? That's got to be against hooker/client privilege or something! Well, I'll never use that agency again!"

Rafe snorted. "You certainly won't," he said before grabbing her by one arm and deftly pulling her over his lap as he sat down on the couch.

"Rafe, no! You can't!" she cried as she frantically tried to roll off his lap.

He simply tucked her in close and began to rain hard swats down on her skirt-covered bottom. His hand fell hard and fast with no discernible rhythm.

"Ohhh... owwww... ouch... please, Rafe..." she yelped as he held her easily in place and thoroughly heated her bottom.

"Are you about ready to go stand in the corner with your naughty bottom on display, young lady?" he asked almost conversationally. "Bear in mind that your punishment hasn't even begun. This is just about standing in the corner right now."

Maxine's breath hissed out in a gasp and then her voice came very soft and tremble-y. "May I go to the corner now?"

Rafe immediately lifted her to stand in front of him. "Are you ready to mind me?"

Her chin quivered as she nodded and looked down into his eyes. "Yes, sir."

He nodded and, never breaking eye contact, worked her skirt up over her hips and bottom until he was able to tuck it into her waistband, then he pulled her panties down to mid-thigh and turned her with another hard swat to her already pink posterior. "To the corner with you, young lady, and I expect those panties to stay exactly where they are."

"Yes, sir." Maxine walked to her bedroom with a little slump to her shoulders, but he had also noticed relief in her eyes that he was taking charge of her again.

• • • • • • •

Max let her breath out in a shuddering sigh as she took her position in the corner. It was odd; though she'd fought him on it, she felt more at peace right now with a bottom blistering imminent than she had in the entire period he'd been away. It was like the world had been shifted back into its axis and everything was okay now.

Her bottom clenched in anticipation of the hard spanking she knew was coming. Rafe was going to light her tail on fire; Max just hoped when he was finished he would set the rest of her aflame as well.

She'd missed the clarity and relief that came with his control. He would take care of everything… he'd take care of her.

Max heard him behind her as he sat down on the edge of her bed. Any second now and he'd call her out of the corner and take her back over his knee.

Clenching her bottom tightly again, she felt the telltale trickle of moisture between her thighs in response to his dominance.

"Come here, little girl, we have things to discuss, you and I. Don't we?" he asked, his deep voice rolling over her like hot honey, turning her bones to mush.

She moved to stand in front of him, not even trying to cover the damp curls that shielded her secrets from his gaze.

He gently took her arm again and guided her down over his lap, running a hand over her already warmed flesh. "What were you thinking, Maxine?"

"I wasn't thinking about anything but pushing you away, pushing away all the feelings inside me. I know I haven't handled any of this well, Rafe. I'm not proud of myself for that." The words were so softly spoken, Max was sure he had to strain to hear them.

He didn't say anything else. It wasn't necessary; they both knew exactly why she'd landed over his lap. Rafe began to bring his hand down hard and fast, each slap making her gasp and mewl as she jerked over his knee.

The heat filling her bottom quickly grew to immense proportions that had her yelling more loudly as she clutched the bedcovers for something to hold on to. She'd forgotten just how much a spanking hurt!

Still his hand continued to fall, then he began to deliver

several in a row to the exact same spot where her bottom and thigh met on one side until she thought she'd die if his hand fell again, then he moved to the other side and gave it the same treatment.

By the time Rafe stood her in front of him again, she was a mess, tears dripping down her face, mingling with other things she'd rather not think about. It was beyond embarrassing to sob like a little girl.

Rafe simply held a handkerchief up to her face. "Blow."

Max did as requested and then he gently mopped her face up before turning her back to the corner. "Now I want you to stand there and consider your behavior since I got back and how you should have handled things differently, because we both know I didn't abandon you; so you need to focus on the real reason you've been pushing me away. You have fifteen minutes, then we'll finish your spanking with a paddling."

Maxine's stomach hit her knees as she looked over her shoulder at him in alarm. "I... er... umm... Rafe, I... I sort of threw away the paddle..."

He grinned. "I suspected as much; don't worry, baby, I brought a replacement. I bought it in Washington right after you hung up on me."

"Oh..." she said rather lamely.

"Yes, oh," Rafe said before twirling his fingers to indicate she needed to face the corner.

Max turned to the corner with a shuddering sigh; as much as she hated the corner, her bottom was grateful for the brief respite. As she stood there with her burning bottom on display and thought about the last few months away from Rafe, she began to cry again. She cried over how much she'd missed him and how worried she'd been about his safe return. When she contemplated how she'd behaved since she'd seen him again, big heaving sobs began to shake her frame.

She'd been completely horrid; she loved this man but she'd treated him as if she hated him. After the first month

Max had begun to focus on the danger of his mission and not knowing exactly where he was in the world. The thought of him coming back with missing pieces—or worse, in a body bag—had consumed her to the point she'd stopped eating and sleeping. Soon she was losing herself in vodka and the dance floor. Somewhere along the line Max managed to convince herself nothing they shared had been real or meant anything to Rafe at all. How could it have meant something if he was able to leave so easily?

She'd nurtured the little thread of doubt until it had grown into bitterness and resentment, and then she'd started acting the part of the woman scorned.

Underneath it all though, her need and love for him had waited... waited until Rafe was home to bring it back into full bloom.

He'd come home to rudeness and an attempt to use him for sex without strings and then she'd hired a prostitute to put him off. What if after all of this and the punishment was over, he decided she wasn't worth the trouble?

As she continued to stand there with harsh sobs wracking her body, she didn't hear him come up behind her until his big warm hands covered her shoulders and turned her into the comfort of his embrace.

"Shhh, baby, everything is going to be okay. I promise, once we finish your punishment, all will be forgiven. Actually you're already forgiven, but I am still going to paddle your naughty bottom for being so audacious and hiring a male escort," he said, pushing her back from him a bit so he could tip her chin up and force her to meet his stern gaze. "I intend to make sure you realize the folly of your actions and never do something like that again."

"I promise I won't, Rafe!" she said fervently. "I wish I hadn't done it this time!"

"You certainly won't. The remembered sting of the Lexan paddle will make sure you think twice before you do anything so foolish. Let's get this done; bend over the end of the bed."

Max moved almost eagerly into place. She needed the punishment to be over so she could be held securely in his arms once more.

A firm hand rested in the small of her back and then the paddle landed with a crisp swat and the most awesome sting she'd ever felt biting into her left bottom cheek. Her mouth formed a little 'o' but no sound escaped until the third swat fell and the sound came out in a full-fledged howl of distress.

She began to buck her hips in an effort to escape the relentless sting; Rafe held her easily in place as he brought the paddle down hard and fast, alternating sides.

"The last six are all going on your sit spots," he told her just before the hardest swat yet fell on her left sit spot with two more following quickly in its wake in the exact same spot. Max tried to pull herself up the bed to escape the horrid paddle, but a hand catching the top of her shoulder prevented that and her right sit spot received the exact same treatment.

She was too busy sobbing and absorbing the intense sting filling her poor posterior to pay much attention to the fact that it was over and Rafe just continued to hold her in place rubbing soothing circles on her back and murmuring to her until she calmed.

Then he sat down on the bed and lifted her to straddle him. Max wrapped her legs instinctively around his hips and gasped when she realized he'd freed himself from his jeans and his cock was pressing insistently at her wet core.

His strong hands cupped her stinging bottom, eliciting a gasp from her as he impaled her on his thick cock. Rafe easily lifted her up and brought her back down hard and fast.

"Who do you belong to, Maxine?" he asked sternly as he continued to pump her up and down his shaft in a relentless rhythm, squeezing her sore bottom with each thrust.

"You!" she cried out in a gasping wail as the pain and pleasure intermingled, flooding her with sensation almost too intense to bear. The orgasm came over her so suddenly that she screamed, and still he continued to work her up and down his shaft, relentlessly wringing another hard orgasm from her before lifting her free of him and bending her over the bed.

Max could only yowl in pleasure when he spread her apart from behind and speared her with his tongue as he worked her clit between two fingers. She tried to shy away when his thumb began to press insistently against her bottom hole, but he pulled her hand away and delivered four sharp swats to her still stinging bottom.

"You will take everything I give you, young lady. Next time I have to use this paddle on your naughty little ass, it will be my cock you feel inside it," Rafe told her firmly as he once again pressed his thumb against her shy little hole. "Relax and let me in."

She whimpered but tried to press her bottom back against his thumb; there was a burning stretch and then his thumb pressed all the way inside while his fingers worked her little clit. Max found herself grinding back on his thumb as the slight pain gave away to pleasure, and then his tongue was thrusting back into her wet heat in tandem with the thumb working its way in and out of her ass.

"Rafe!" she cried passionately as she came apart under his hands and mouth. Then he slid up her body, keeping his thumb firmly seated in her ass, surrounding her with his heat as he drove his throbbing cock back inside her pulsing channel to the hilt with one hard thrust.

Max felt impossibly full with his thick cock slamming into her and his thumb filling her ass. She was stretched to the limit, and the pleasure was so intense she was afraid she wouldn't survive the next orgasm.

Rafe pounded her hard, every slam of his hips making contact against her punished bottom and reawakening the sting, but she reveled in every pain as it intertwined with the pleasure.

When his fingers pressed her swollen clit down so his

cock abraded it and shoved it back against his fingers with every hard thrust, she came screaming his name yet again in an orgasm that seemed to go on and on.

By the time he shouted her name into the back of her neck, she was moaning in helpless pleasure, her body shuddering and shivering beneath him. With one final thrust he ground tight against her, sending her into another spasm of delight as she felt the heat of his seed fill her and splash against her inner walls.

He had taken her hard, and she winced when he pulled free from her.

Max would have gotten up but Rafe pressed her back into the bed. "Stay where you are."

With a weary sigh of contentment she did as she was told. Then he was back, gently cleaning her with a warm cloth before stripping her dress over her head, making her embarrassingly aware that they had moved from spanking to sex without removing their clothes. Her bra joined the dress on the floor, and then he quickly stripped before lifting her in his arms to lay her down in the center of the bed, climbing in after her, and wrapping her in his arms.

Max wrapped her arms around his where they held her and pushed her tender bottom into his stomach and her back tight against his chest; tangling the fingers of one hand with his, she pulled both their hands up to her face so she could kiss his. "I'm so glad you're home and holding me in your arms again."

"This is where you belong, Maxine… where you will always belong," he told her. "Go to sleep, baby. We'll talk more in the morning."

"Yes, sir," Max said with a yawn as her eyes began to drift closed.

# CHAPTER TEN

Max woke to the feel of Rafe spreading her wide and sinking into her slowly until his scrotum was flush against her.

She groaned and arched her back in an effort to encourage him to move, but he stayed still.

"Look at me, Maxine," his dark voice commanded. Max looked up and found herself caught in the intensity of his gaze.

As soon as their eyes met he began to move; he took her with slow hard thrusts, never taking his eyes from hers.

Soon she was doing her best to speed him up as he continued the maddeningly slow pace, pulling out almost completely inch by inch and then coming back inside just as slowly until he pressed against her again. Each time he was all the way inside her he rotated his hips, grinding against her until she was about to come, but then he started his slow withdrawal again, removing the delicious pressure before she could go over the edge.

Max began to whimper, closing her eyes and turning her head away in frustration, only to have him cup her face firmly in his hands with his elbows planted on either side of her head. "Look at me."

Her eyes sprang back open to meet his eyes once more; her reward for obedience was four fast hard thrusts before he began the relentlessly slow rhythm again.

"Don't look away from me," Rafe said firmly.

"Please... Rafe... I need..." Max begged softly, desperate for the release she knew he could give her.

"Soon, baby... soon... who do you belong to, Maxine?" he asked her as he increased his rhythm ever so slightly.

"You! I belong to you!" she cried, gasping out the words as his pace continued to increase.

"Yes... you belong to me! Who do I belong to?" Rafe asked, grinding his pelvic bone against her clit as he voiced the question.

"Me! You belong to me!" Max cried out as he began to pound in and out of her hard and fast, still never breaking eye contact. Max felt as if he were seeing into her very soul.

"That's right, baby. You belong to me... I belong to you... we belong to each other forever. Don't ever forget that again!" he said sternly, suddenly thrusting into her hard enough to push her up the bed as he hammered in and out.

Max screamed as her orgasm washed over her. She couldn't do anything but cling to his shoulders and wrap her legs around his waist as he continued the pounding rhythm. Then he pressed his forehead against hers and pressed in as deep as he could go and began to grind against her in a circular motion.

Everything inside her began to shake and tighten as he continued to press hard and rub against something deep inside her. "Rafe!"

"That's it, baby... come for me again... Now!" he growled, and her back arched and every muscle in her body seemed to clamp down as she exploded around him in the most intense orgasm she'd ever experienced. It seemed to go on and on until she fell back on the bed in a boneless heap and Rafe shuddered his own release above her.

As she came back down to earth, wrapped safe in Rafe's arms, Max began to cry, partly from the intensity of what they'd just shared but also because of what she'd come perilously close to throwing away.

A big hand came up to cup the back of her head as Rafe rolled to his back; bringing her with him, he pressed her face to his chest. "Shhh... everything's okay, I've got you, baby girl."

"I'm so... sorry, Rafe... so sorry..." she sobbed into his chest.

"Honey, we dealt with this last night. Everything's forgiven. You're okay, I'm okay, and most important, we're okay. I've got you, honey, and I promise I'll never let you go again," he said firmly as he lifted her chin and kissed away her tears.

"I love you, Rafe," Max said earnestly as she looked down into his eyes.

He grinned and lightly smacked her still tender backside. "And don't you forget it!"

"Yes, sir," she said with a saucy grin as he rolled her back beneath him.

## CHAPTER ELEVEN

Max smiled as she stood at the copier; almost everything in her world was back to normal and pretty close to perfect.

A sharp pain hit her in the side that made her catch her breath with a frown. The pains that were becoming more and more frequent were the only fly in her ointment. She knew she needed to go to the doctor but wasn't looking forward to hearing what he had to say.

She'd been a few months ago when the pains first started and he'd told her she was working on an ulcer in her stomach. He'd gone on to tell her she needed to stop drinking immediately and start eating a healthy but bland diet. Advice she'd ignored and now she was paying the price.

"Why are you holding your side? Did you have another pain?" She jumped at the sound of Rafe's voice behind her.

"It's nothing, honey," she said with a smile. "I'm fine."

He frowned. "I think we need to get you checked out by the doctor; you're grabbing your side with those pains far too often."

"It's nothing, I'm sure," she argued.

"Maxine, you big fibber!" Renee, her friend and drinking buddy was suddenly standing next to them.

"Renee, really… there's no need to involve yourself in

this discussion…"

A firm hand clamped down on her arm in warning as Rafe pulled her into his side. "What is she fibbing about, Renee?"

Renee blushed under Rafe's intense scrutiny, but then turned to frown at Maxine. "I'm sorry, Max, but the doctor told you two months ago to start eating right and stop drinking because you were developing an ulcer. You haven't done anything he suggested despite my asking you to stop drinking vodka like water."

Max looked at the floor nervously as she felt Rafe's intense regard shift back to her. "This really isn't anyone's business, Renee," she said sharply.

"This is the business of anyone who cares about you. Apologize to your friend and thank her for her concern."

"I won't! She had no business blurting my business out and broadcasting it to the office at large!" Max yelled with a stamp of her foot.

"I apologize for my fiancée's rudeness and am very thankful to you for bringing this to my attention, Renee. I promise Maxine will be thanking you and giving her apologies once she's had time to think about it," Rafe said with an assurance that made Max's bottom tingle in alarm as he turned and began to escort her toward the front of the office.

Rafe stuck his head in Tom's office. "Maxine and I will be out for the rest of the day. She needs to see her doctor and then we still have a few things to settle between us."

"No problem, Rafe. I'm glad you're back. See you both tomorrow," Tom said with a smile.

Rafe said nothing as he escorted her to his truck and helped her inside. Max began to chew nervously on her lower lip. He was being way too quiet.

"It's not like I'm not capable of handling my own business," she muttered under her breath.

"Apparently you haven't been handling this at all… you've just been ignoring it. Am I right, young lady?" he asked succinctly.

Max swallowed. "I was depressed and I missed you so bad and…"

"This is a yes or no question, Maxine. Did you or did you not ignore the doctor's advice?"

She sighed in defeat. "Yes, sir."

"We will be discussing this at length later but now, what's the address of your doctor's office?" Rafe asked her in a tone that brooked no argument.

Knowing she had no real choice, Max gave him the address; it was embarrassing to have her boyfriend taking her to the doctor like a naughty child. Boyfriend… at the office Rafe had called her his fiancée…

"Rafe, you called me your fiancée…"

"I did," he said matter-of-factly.

"Well… um, don't you have to ask me a question before you can call me that?" she asked with the beginnings of her the first smile she'd had since those pains hit at the copier.

"I don't have any intention of asking you anything, young lady. I love you… you love me… we're getting married… end of story. But I wouldn't worry about it right now if I were you. You have enough to worry about between the doctor and me."

Max frowned; this was going to be a long day.

• • • • • • •

Max chewed her lower lip as the doctor pressed firmly down on her abdomen, frowning every time she winced. The situation wasn't helped by the fact that Rafe had followed them into the exam room and stood glowering down at her from his position next to the exam table.

"You've definitely gotten worse. Did you take any of the medications I prescribed?" the doctor asked with a scowl.

Max opened her mouth but Rafe interrupted to ask her, "Did you even have them filled?"

She looked down and shook her head no, suddenly a

little ashamed of herself.

The doctor made a tsking sound. "Why are you here if you have no intention of following my directions?"

"She will follow all your instructions to the letter from this point on, doctor. I promise you that," Rafe said with a stern look at Max.

"She will need to eat three healthy meals a day and her diet will need to be fairly bland until her stomach and intestines recover from the abuse she's given them," the doctor said.

"Not a problem, doctor. If she fails to do so, she will stand to eat," Rafe said succinctly.

Max gasped and felt her face turn bright red.

The doctor turned to study Rafe thoughtfully. "You will ensure she takes care of herself from now on?"

"I will. Miss Maxine will toe a very narrow line with regards to her health from this point forward," Rafe assured the doctor.

"Rafe, I can handle this without…" Max tried to interject.

"If you'd been handling it, none of this would be occurring," Rafe said firmly before turning his attention back to the doctor.

"I will give you prescriptions for Nexium and Carafate. The Carafate will be temporary. It will help to coat the lining of her stomach while it heals. The Nexium will reduce her acid levels and also help with healing and protecting her stomach from future damage," the doctor explained. Max glared up at both of them from her position on the table. They were discussing her as if she weren't even in the room.

"I would like to administer a medicinal enema before you leave. It's a mixture I've developed that will help to soothe the lining of her intestines to get a jumpstart on the healing process while cleansing the rest of the toxins from her alcohol consumption from her system."

Max sat straight up on the table. "I don't think so! Not happening!"

A large hand pressed her back down on the table as Rafe leaned over her. "You will do whatever the good doctor deems necessary, young lady. You can either cooperate now or you can cooperate in a few minutes with a bright red bottom for the doctor to look at while he gives you the enema. Your choice."

Max closed her eyes against the implacability in Rafe's face. She felt tears gathering as she realized she was going to have to submit to an enema. The situation was embarrassing enough without adding a spanking in front of the doctor; it was bad enough he'd made it very clear he spanked her regularly.

The doctor cleared his throat. "I cannot of course force you to have the enema, Maxine, but I do feel it would be in your best interest."

Max sighed and gave in to the inevitable. "I'll take the enema."

"Please strip from the waist down and put this sheet over your lap. I'll go prepare my supplies and return with a nurse," he instructed before leaving the room.

"This is the most mortifying situation I've ever been in," Max complained as she pulled off her skirt and underwear before climbing back up on the table with the flimsy plastic sheet over her lap and tucked around her hips.

"A situation of your own making, young lady," Rafe pointed out with a growl.

Max decided to study the floor rather than looking at Rafe; maybe if she didn't make eye contact for the rest of the visit, she could pretend none of this was happening.

The doctor was back before too much time passed along with a sour-faced nurse who was carrying a huge bag of fluid and a bunch of rolled-up tubing. The end of the tube protruding from her gloved hand had a large broad nozzle attached to it, and Max realized that was the part that was going up her butt. She groaned at the sight of it.

"Now, young lady, if you'll roll over onto your side..." the doctor began.

"I have a better idea," Rafe interrupted. Max squeaked when he suddenly picked her up and laid her face down on the table with her legs hanging off the end at a ninety-degree angle.

"Rafe!" she cried out in protest, only to gasp when a sharp swat landed on her left bottom cheek.

"I think this is the best way to ensure this never needs to be repeated. A little embarrassment will do her good," Rafe said firmly and then to her horror he cupped a bottom cheek and spread her wide for the good doctor.

"Hmmmm... well... perhaps you're right," the doctor said and Max winced when she heard the snap of his gloves on his wrist. Then she felt the firm pressure of the slippery nozzle pressing against her shy little hole.

"Relax your bottom, Maxine," Rafe said sternly.

She whimpered but found herself responding to his instructions and relaxed as the nozzle slid deep inside her ass.

"Very good," the doctor said and then she heard the sound as he released the valve on the enema bag and warm fluid began to flood into her bowels.

Max groaned as the warm liquid filled her insides. It was strangely soothing and uncomfortable at the same time, and it seemed to go on and on until she thought she'd explode if they tried to get any more of it into her. Then the doctor murmured something that sounded suspiciously like 'good girl' under his breath and removed the nozzle.

"I need to go to the bathroom," Max said as a spasm hit her bowels.

"I'm afraid you need to hold the medicine for at least ten minutes before evacuating," the doctor said.

"I can't!" Max wailed.

"Yes, you can, Maxine, I'll help you." Rafe told her, soothingly placing his big hand over her bottom and cupping it possessively.

"Yes, well, we'll step out into the hall. As soon as the ten minutes are up you can help her into the attached bathroom, clean up, and meet me in my office to get the prescriptions."

Max breathed a sigh of relief when the door closed behind the doctor and his nurse. One thing was for certain—she was never coming back to this doctor's office again. Not only had Rafe threatened her with a spanking, he'd held her bottom open for an enema; she never wanted to make eye contact with the doctor or his nurse again.

Her stomach continued to cramp, but Rafe's hand stayed on her ass, oddly reassuring her while he began rubbing her back soothingly with his other hand. They didn't talk, and Max was thankful for that. She wished she thought Rafe would see this entire office visit as punishment enough, but she knew better.

Finally her ten minutes was up and Rafe removed his finger and helped her to the bathroom where he washed his hands while she took care of business. He didn't say one word while she cleaned up and dressed, which made Max's nervousness grow by leaps and bounds.

In no time at all they had her prescriptions in hand and they were alone in his truck. Max looked at his unhappy profile and suppressed a shudder. She was in big trouble.

"Please don't be mad at me," she said nervously from the seat next to him.

"Don't be mad at you? Maxine, you've been neglecting your health for months," he said incredulously. "Something that stops as of now."

"I don't think I was neglecting my health really..."

"You didn't even get the medicine filled to help heal your stomach!" Rafe said with no little exasperation.

She sniffled a little and ducked her head. "I'm sorry, Rafe. It just didn't seem important."

"You're going to be sorry, young lady. Once we've gotten your medicine and I get you home, you're going to be one very sorry young lady indeed."

"Yes, sir," she said softly.

Max sat quietly in her seat as they pulled up to the pharmacy drive-through; thankfully the line was empty and her meds were ready so it was a quick stop. She started to get out of the car when they stopped at the grocery store, but Rafe waved her back to her seat.

"You stay here and think about why you're in so much trouble. I just need to grab something from produce," he said firmly.

She wasn't sure why but somehow the way he said produce seemed foreboding. He was back in a few minutes with a relatively small bag she found herself eyeing nervously.

As they walked into the apartment, Rafe turned to her and said, "You go take a shower while I make dinner. Put on a loose gown and no panties then come to the table."

Rafe's quiet anger was far more unsettling than it would have been if he was yelling at her. Max found herself hurrying though her shower and quickly drying off before putting on a loose gown.

Max was extremely conscious of her bare bottom beneath the gown as she walked to the kitchen to join Rafe. He was setting a bowl of macaroni and cheese with ham in front of her place as she came into the room, but it was the glass of water with a big round root sitting in it that drew her attention. It looked kind of like a potato carved into an almost phallic shape, though not as wide as an actual penis.

"What is that?" she asked nervously, as she pondered where he planned to put the big white root.

"I'm glad you asked," he said almost conversationally. "It's ginger root. Among its many purposes, ginger root is also very good at delivering a much-needed lesson to naughty bottoms."

Her eyes shot wide in alarm. "Bottoms?"

"Yes, ma'am, you heard me correctly. Now lift your gown and bend over the edge of the table," Rafe instructed firmly.

"But... Rafe, I..." she stammered nervously.

"Now." The quietly voiced command had her scrambling into place.

# UNACCEPTABLE BEHAVIOR

"I'm sorry... I'll..."

"Right now all I want you to do is mind me. Reach back and hold your bottom cheeks apart for me," he said in a tone that warned argument would not be viewed favorably.

With a little whimper, Max reached back and pulled her bottom cheeks apart, trying not to think about the view she was providing.

"Good girl," Rafe said, putting a warm palm on the small of her back as he pressed the head of the root against her tightly clenched bottom hole. "Relax and bear down to make it easier, baby. Don't fight against it," he advised.

"Ohhh..." Max panted, bearing down and gasping as the tip of the root began to slip inside the tight ring of her anus. The stretch and burn of its intrusion was immediate.

Rafe continued applying steady pressure as the head of the root sank inside, then he backed it out slowly and worked it back in over and over again, getting more inside her with each inward stroke.

"Please... no more, Rafe... I'll be good, I promise," she wailed as the juices of the ginger began to sink into the flesh of her anus, adding to the burn exponentially.

"You will definitely be a good girl, I plan to make sure of it," he said firmly as he finally sank the root past the broader base to the groove he'd carved to hold it in place, leaving a broader part about an inch long protruding from between her bottom cheeks. Once it was in place to his satisfaction, he patted her bottom lightly. "Now sit down and eat your dinner."

Max stood up and flinched as her bottom tightened down on the intruder and released more of its fiery essence into her ass. "Oohh... Rafe, it burns! I can't sit down!"

"You will sit down in that chair and eat your dinner, young lady. Right now," he said with not an ounce of softness in his gaze.

Max sat down carefully in her chair and groaned as the action pressed the root deeper inside. The burn seemed to grow with every minute, making her shift continuously in her seat.

Her appetite completely gone, Max was only able to eat about half of her bowl of macaroni and cheese before she pushed it away miserably. "I can't eat anymore."

Rafe studied her features and then gave a nod as he simply handed her two pills. "Swallow your medicine then go to the bedroom. I expect to find you standing with your nose in the corner totally naked."

"Naked?" she asked, alarmed. Though he'd seen her naked body on several occasions, the thought of waiting naked in a corner with a plug of ginger sticking out of her ass was too mortifying to contemplate.

"Little girl, you've got one hell of a hiding coming. If you want I can spank you now until you agree to do as I've asked, but it won't change what you've already got coming. It's up to you."

Max pulled her gown over her head and dropped it in front of him on the kitchen floor and then walked proudly to the bedroom. Well, as proudly as she could hobbling with a stick up her ass. She didn't wait around to see what he thought of her small show of attitude.

She put her nose in the corner with a sniff, trying to ignore the awful burn in her asshole and the embarrassing wetness increasing in other areas.

• • • • • • •

Rafe almost laughed when she stripped in the kitchen and sailed out with the bearing of a haughty queen. The little wink of ginger between her ass cheeks detracted only slightly from the image.

His girl had definite spirit and he wouldn't want her any other way. It was too bad she had such a harsh lesson to learn but her lack of care of herself had to be addressed. She could have caused herself serious harm if she'd continued down her current path and possibly even killed herself.

This was one lesson he planned to deliver in no

uncertain terms to ensure it never had to be repeated.

He walked into the bedroom to find her as instructed with her nose pressed to the corner; as he watched her, she shifted from one foot to another, probably partly due to nerves and partly due to the ginger stinging her tender little hole. He was about to increase the burn in a memorable way.

Rafe sat down on the corner of the bed. "Come here."

Maxine's shoulders slumped with dejection as she turned slowly to face him and walked toward him with halting steps. "I'm sorry."

"You soon will be," he said firmly, holding out a hand to her.

She took his hand as if grateful for the assistance in those last few steps.

"Why are we here, Maxine?"

She took a deep breath. "I haven't been taking care of myself."

"And?" he asked with a quirked brow.

"I didn't follow doctor's orders and get my prescriptions filled. I know I should have, Rafe. I'm really sorry," she said softly.

"Sometimes sorry isn't enough, baby. I take the health and well-being of the woman I love very seriously. I'm about to show you just how seriously," he said as he pulled her down over his left leg and clamped his right one down over her bare thighs, leaving her to dangle helplessly with her hands braced on the floor.

He ran his hand lightly over the soft smooth flesh of her upturned bottom. "I'm going to give you a long hard spanking with my hand and then you will bring me the Lexan paddle and ask me to finish your spanking."

"Yes, sir," she said with a slight whimper.

"Now ask for your spanking," he instructed.

"Please, will you spank me?" she asked.

"Spank you how?"

"Please, will you spank me on my bare bottom?" Maxine

shuddered again over his thigh as the words left her.

Rafe lifted his right hand high and then brought it down hard on her left cheek, making her jerk with a gasp. Pulling her in tight, he began to slap down hard, alternating cheeks as he watched the color bloom brightly in her backside.

He began bringing his hand down harder and faster until she couldn't contain her soft cries. When her ass was a satisfying shade of red, he tilted her forward a little and began to spank her sit spots. He brought his hand down over and over in the exact same spot on her left side until she was almost sobbing.

"Please… not in the same place… I'll be good… I promise!" she cried desperately, sighing in relief when he moved to the right side. Her relief was short-lived when the right side got the exact same treatment.

"Rafe, please!" she yelled just as he stilled his hand and let it rest on the hot skin of her well-spanked behind.

He let her hang there over his knee for a few minutes until her breathing slowed and he knew she was calm, and lifted her to stand in front of him again. Rafe caught her hands when they immediately moved to rub her stinging bottom. "No rubbing."

Big tears dripped down her cheeks as she stood before him with her little chin quivering. "Please forgive me."

Rafe smiled sadly and used his thumb to wipe away a tear. "You were forgiven already, baby, but that doesn't change your punishment. What do you need to do now?"

Maxine drew herself up with resolve and moved to the dresser to get the Lexan paddle, stiffening her shoulders as she brought it to him. "Please, sir, will you paddle my bottom to finish my punishment?"

"The paddling will finish your spanking but the punishment won't be quite over, little girl," he said sternly.

Her mouth opened in a sweet little 'o' of surprise. "Wh-what?"

"What did I tell you would happen the next time I had to use the Lexan paddle on your naughty bottom? What did

I say happens to naughty girls who need a paddling?" Rafe asked.

A red almost as bright as her bottom spread slowly up her neck and into her cheeks. "You said… you said the next time you used the paddle you would… I would…"

"Yes?"

"You said I would take your cock up my ass." She rushed through the words as if saying them fast would make it better somehow.

"That's right, naughty young ladies get their little bottoms punished inside and out, and your tight little spanked ass is going to feel so good around my cock." He said the words to add to her embarrassment and it worked as evidenced by the red staining her face and neck. "Bend over and grab your ankles."

• • • • • • •

Max bent over and grabbed her ankles; she was reeling from embarrassment but also found herself aching with need. His words, his dominance had moisture leaking like a fountain from between her legs. She knew he could see everything with her bent over like this, the plug wagging at him like a lewd little tail and the wetness on her lips dripping to her thighs… he could see it all. She was mortified and more turned on than ever before.

"You're getting ten swats to each sit spot," Rafe's deep voice spoke from behind her, the position she was in and the plug in her bottom made it impossible to clench her bottom.

He didn't make her wait; the first searing swat landed almost immediately on her left sit spot, followed quickly by the next in the same spot. She wailed as she realized he was going to deliver each and every swat to the exact same place before he moved on to the other side.

Max knew he wasn't paddling as hard as he could but each and every stroke of the thin paddle made it feel like he was branding her with a hot iron. As she wagged her bottom from side to side in response, the stinging inside her bottom from the well-placed ginger seemed to grow in direct proportion to the heat in her seat.

By the time he moved to the right side, she was openly sobbing. Mercifully he didn't seem inclined to draw the paddling out and he finished the remaining ten swats quickly, each swat landing hard and fast in the exact same place on her right sit spot. When it was over, she held her position, needing a minute as the heat in her ass seemed to continue to grow.

Then two fingers plunged into her wet sheath without warning and her knees nearly buckled at the intense pleasure meshing with her pain. "Ooooh!!"

She eagerly moved her legs apart in an effort to get him to delve deeper. Rafe obliged her by adding a third finger and thrusting them in and out of her hard and fast until she was about to go over the edge into bliss. But before she could completely go over, he stopped and removed the fingers.

"I'm not sure my naughty girl deserves to come," he said musingly as she rose and tuned to face him just in time to see him cleaning her essence from his fingers with his tongue.

Her knees almost buckled as he licked his fingers clean with obvious enjoyment. Her muscles clamped down on emptiness, increasing the ache in her core. She needed him so badly.

"Bend over the end of the bed again and hold yourself open for me," he instructed.

Max bent over the bed, shivering with a mix of anticipation and fear as she reached back, caught a sore bottom cheek in each hand, and spread herself wide. She felt the press of his legs against her as he caught the end of the root plug and worked it slowly in and out of her a few times before pulling it free.

The sound of it hitting the trashcan next to the bed as

he tossed it in distracted her for a moment before she heard the tearing of a foil packet. He was really going to do it… he was going to take her ass! Max buried her face in the bed and waited.

Then came the insistent press of the head of his cock against her tender orifice. Max whimpered as her tight little hole stretched around him, burning, but Rafe forged forward with gentle determination. He eased in a few inches and then back out, claiming more of her ass with each thrust until he was seated fully inside her and she felt the press of his balls against her.

The heat and burn from the ginger was different from the burn of the cock stretching her most private place wide open; as he held still to let her get accustomed to the feel of him, Max found she wanted to grind back against him.

She needed more; Max wriggled experimentally and apparently that was all Rafe had been waiting for because he withdrew and thrust back inside quickly, making her pant with need.

His first few thrusts were careful, but as she rocked back against him, he began to take her hard. Rafe reached around her, caught her throbbing little clit between his thumb and forefinger, and milked it firmly as he pounded into her ass.

Max's first orgasm came on so fast, she bucked uncontrollably beneath him on the bed as everything inside her tightened and released hard but still he rode her.

"That's it, baby, you feel so good around my cock. So tight and hot; come for me again."

Using his other hand, he thrust three fingers deep inside her empty core and began to work them in and out in tandem with his cock as his other hand continued to work her clit relentlessly.

She began to wail as the pain in her punished bottom, the burn from the ginger, her throbbing clit, and the double penetration washed her in an overload sensation. Pain became pleasure and pleasure became need. "Please! Rafe, please… harder… faster… oooh!"

Soon all she could do was scream her pleasure as she came again and again with no respite until finally he shouted his own release into the back of her neck and they both collapsed to the mattress.

Max gave a small cry of pain when he withdrew from her well-used ass, but stayed where she was face down on the bed, too sated and exhausted from the punishment and pleasure to move.

She heard him cleaning up in the bathroom and then he was back cleaning her up with a warm washcloth before scooping her in his arms and laying her down in the middle of the bed.

Max sighed with contentment when he climbed in behind her and curved his body protectively around hers as he pulled the covers over them.

Rafe placed a gentle kiss on the tip of her ear and whispered, "Who do you belong to?"

"You, Rafe, you, always you," she said softly as she stroked the arm wrapped around her middle.

"Who do I belong to?" he asked.

Max felt a smile bloom across her face as the reality of the lesson came through and the knowledge filled her with peace. "You belong to me."

"That's right, baby. We belong to each other, forever and always. I might piss you off from time to time and you will definitely piss me off, but that will never change. I'm not going anywhere and I don't plan to ever let you go anywhere either. Understood?"

"Understood."

# EPILOGUE

Max smiled as they entered the reception hall. The wedding had been everything she'd ever dreamed of, and Rafe was the perfect groom.

In the past six months she'd gained back all the weight she'd lost while Rafe was gone, along with the curves he so adored. She was healthy and they were happy.

The only bad part of the wedding was the night before when he'd introduced her to his best man at the rehearsal. To say she was shocked to see Javier, the escort she'd hired six months ago, was an understatement. Finding out he was actually a member of Rafe's black ops team and that she'd been under surveillance the entire time he'd been in the Middle East was another shock.

She'd torn into both men with gusto. Max didn't care if it was protocol or not—Rafe could have told her she was being watched! The fact that Javier, aka Jake Robulard, had posed as her hired escort didn't exactly endear the man to her either.

Jake had explained he'd only been looking after Rafe and making sure he and his lady were okay. But that hadn't helped—it had sent Max straight over the edge.

Max told both Rafe and Jake in no uncertain terms that

if she wanted to hire an escort, then she would do so without any further interference from either of them.

Rafe had interfered immediately, excusing them from the bridal party and taking her into a back office of the church, where he'd turned her over his knee and spanked her soundly before spinning her around and kissing her senseless. "No more escorts, ever!"

Max had smiled up at her Neanderthal, her backside burning. "Yes, sir," she whispered before pulling his mouth back down to hers.

The wedding had gone off without a hitch and now they were about to celebrate their union surrounded by their family and friends. Jake and Renee had hit it off and were already on the dance floor when she and Rafe arrived.

Rafe pulled her close on the dance floor and Max smiled dreamily up at him. No one else knew she was dancing around in her wedding dress without panties. That was a secret between her and the groom along with the red bottom he'd given her just before they left for the church. He said it was to remind her what the consequences were if she chose not to obey like she promised in her vows, but Max had a sneaking suspicion it was to ensure she was ready to jump his bones as soon as they left the reception.

But it didn't matter what the reason was. Rafe's discipline grounded her and gave her a sense of being loved and cared for she'd never known before, and she knew she'd love him for the rest of her days. He was her hero.

# THE END

STORMY NIGHT PUBLICATIONS WOULD LIKE TO THANK
YOU FOR YOUR INTEREST IN OUR BOOKS.

If you liked this book (or even if you didn't), we would really appreciate you leaving a review on the site where you purchased it. Reviews provide useful feedback for us and for our authors, and this feedback (both positive comments and constructive criticism) allows us to work even harder to make sure we provide the content our customers want to read.

If you would like to check out more books from Stormy Night Publications, if you want to learn more about our company, or if you would like to join our mailing list, please visit our website at:

www.stormynightpublications.com

Made in the USA
Lexington, KY
11 February 2018